Cade might have seen the steer first if he hadn't taken Hula Girl on ahead. But it was Baxter, new to being a cutting horse, who sighted the steer and jolted Darby from her daydream of wild stallions.

Unlike the red Hereford cattle they'd been herding, this steer's coat was a mix of brown, yellow, and black. But the most distinctive thing about him was a crumpled horn.

The broken ends of the horn stuck up, ragged and discolored with dried blood.

That injury has to hurt, Darby guessed. The wandering steer was in no mood to be herded. He might have sensed Baxter's inexperience, too, because he struck his cloven hoof at the grass, then lowered his head.

Baxter snorted and strained against the reins, trying to lower his own head.

"A face-off is not a great idea, Bax," Darby whispered.

Check out the

series, also by Terri Farley!

Phantom Stallion

WILD HORSE ISLAND 9

SNOWFIRE

TERRI FARLEY

HarperTrophy®
An Imprint of HarperCollins*Publishers*

Horse lovers worldwide are grateful to the Wild Horse Preservation League and the Wild Horse Sanctuary for rescuing a wild white stallion so much like the one on this cover. Thanks for saving the real Phantom!

Disclaimer

Wild Horse Island is imaginary. Its history, legends, people, and ecology echo Hawaii's, but my stories and reality are like leaves on the rain-forest floor. They may overlap, but their edges never really match.

Harper Trophy® is a registered trademark
of HarperCollins Publishers.

Library of Congress catalog card number: 2008921073
ISBN 978-0-06-162643-2

❖

First Harper Trophy edition, 2008

9
SNOWFIRE

© Gary Chalk

TWO SISTERS VOLCANOES

MESSAGE
BOTTLE LANDING

RAIN
FOREST

IOLANI
RANCH

SUN
HOUSE

OLD PLANTATION

TUTU'S
COTTAGE

CRIMSON
VALE

NIGHT DIGGER
POINT BEACH

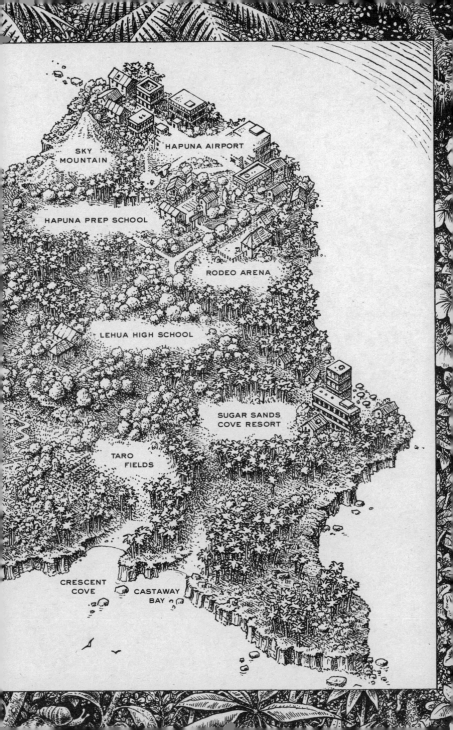

Chapter One

Darby Carter pressed her legs against her stirrup leathers. The blue roan gelding beneath her stepped out into a jog, just as she'd asked, but the herd of red cattle ahead didn't speed up. They scattered.

Ten cows and eight calves didn't amount to a stampede, but Darby loosened her reins, letting Baxter extend his trot. His sudden speed made her black ponytail snap, but the cattle ignored the horse and rider.

"Get back!" Darby raised her right hand from her reins. She wished she had a hat to wave.

Not that Cade was waving his, she thought, glancing at him. The young Hawaiian cowboy rode at the front of the herd with his hala hat pulled down, almost covering his short, tight braid. He rode loose and completely relaxed in the saddle.

When they'd first started out, a calfless cow behind Cade had veered away from the bunch. As if he had eyes in the back of his head, Cade had noticed and signaled Hula Girl, the chestnut cutter he rode, to smoothly block the cow.

Darby's job was to watch for stragglers, but Cade hadn't told her the cattle might spread out and stray in all different directions.

She shot another glance up at Cade. He made this chore look easy. If he knew she was entirely messing up her part of moving the cattle to higher pastures, he didn't show it.

Forget riding loose and relaxed, Darby thought. The only way she could keep the cattle moving forward was by trotting closer to the animals.

Baxter was new at this, but Darby didn't blame the gelding for their awkwardness. Baxter's blueberries-and-cream-colored coat darkened with sweat as he tried to do what she wanted.

As they rode past the broodmare pasture, Darby spotted two foals sparring with each other. First she recognized the tan one, Blue Moon. The foals reared, nipped, and chased each other. As they raced past Lady Wong, the mare's foal, Black Cat, joined the game.

Even though their hooves were so tiny that Darby knew she could enclose one in her hand, the young horses were swift and agile. They swept near the fence and Darby saw the bay foal playing with them was Luna Dancer, Hula Girl's baby.

"He's Mr. Independence," Darby told Baxter, because Luna Dancer had weaned himself ahead of most of the year's foals.

Baxter's ears swiveled, but not to listen to Darby. He snorted with excitement as a calf corkscrewed its skinny tail, then straightened it high in the air before bounding away from the herd.

"Oh, no, you don't," Darby scolded.

The calf actually looked back at her before giving a buck of high spirits. Then he ran.

Should she desert her position at the rear of the herd to pursue the calf?

Baxter flattened his ears and decided for her. As he bolted after the calf, hooves falling in the same dusty zigzag path, Darby crowded against the gelding's neck.

Baxter was so excited, he raced right past the calf. Darby turned him back, trying to block the fugitive calf's escape. Baxter obeyed, making such a tight arc, Darby's left stirrup skidded on dirt.

Her turn wasn't pretty, but it worked. The calf gave a frightened bawl, then ran back to his mother.

Darby gave Baxter's sweaty neck a pat, but the gelding didn't notice. Once more, he was watching the herd.

The cattle mooed, rolled their eyes, and a few

stopped. Others swung their big bodies back toward the ranch.

If the cattle made it back to where they'd started, Darby knew her grandfather, Jonah, and Kimo, a hardworking ranch hand, would turn her lack of skill into a good-natured joke.

What was she doing wrong? She was about to shout her question at Cade when Hula Girl slowed. Leaving the lead to a loud red cow, Cade made his mount drop back along the right side of the herd until she matched steps with Baxter.

"Slow and easy," Cade told Darby. "And quiet."

Hula Girl's gait dropped down to a walk, so Darby slowed Baxter.

Amazingly, the cattle moved back into a calm herd and continued their journey toward Upper Sugar Mill pasture. They walked with purpose, swinging their heads at occasional flies, but they looked relaxed, and Darby couldn't figure out why.

"Don't believe the movies." Cade's voice was so low, Darby strained to hear him.

"Don't believe the movies?" she repeated.

"You could make this herd do what you want them to by sitting over there"—he nodded toward a cinnamon-colored gouge on a green hill at least a mile away—"and raising your hand."

Maybe you could, Darby thought, but she just said, "Okay."

Darby watched Cade ride on back to the head of

the herd, and muffled a cough with her hand. It wasn't her asthma kicking up, just a reaction to the dust, but she was reassured by the feel of her inhaler in her front pocket.

Since she'd come to 'Iolani Ranch three months ago, her asthma had practically disappeared. The clean ocean air on Moku Lio Hihiu—Hawaiian for Wild Horse Island—was a huge improvement over the pollution and smog of Pacific Pinnacles, California.

Even to herself, she'd stopped calling California home.

Surrounded by flowers and birdsong, Darby drifted into thoughts of how much she loved Hawaii. She was convinced she'd landed in exactly the right place in the world. How many other eighth graders were riding up tropical mountainsides during their study breaks?

As a first-year student at Lehua High School, this was the first time she'd faced two-hour-long final exams. She'd had her last full day of classes on Friday, and today she'd gotten off at noon. Tomorrow was "dead day"—meaning a full day of study. And Wednesday finals began.

When Baxter tried to lope up the hill, Darby tightened her reins and kept him at a walk.

"To save your legs," she muttered to the gelding, but that wasn't the only reason. Baxter had to know what was expected of him. She couldn't just be a lump along for the ride.

When they finally reached the entrance to Upper Sugar Mill pasture, Darby smiled. The cattle milled impatiently. They'd recognized the place and bumped against the fence, eager to get inside and sample the fresh pasture.

Darby lifted her shoulder to let her T-shirt blot a drop of sweat that had trailed down her cheek, then sighed and sat back against her saddle cantle. They'd made it.

Cade swung Hula Girl alongside the gate and slid the bolt, opening the gate from the saddle. Then he nodded.

Darby hesitated at his signal, and Cade said, "Take 'em on in."

With Baxter at a flat-footed walk behind them, the cattle shoved through the opening.

Wide spans of grass rolled over mounds of earth and down slopes, rising and falling in search of the horizon where the Two Sisters volcanoes wore leis of cloud.

Beyond, the grass turned dark emerald as it surrounded Sky Mountain. Today the farthest peak looked like an upside-down golden cone topped with vanilla ice cream.

The cattle had just fanned out and fallen to grazing when Jack and Jill, two of the ranch's five Australian shepherds, trotted over a hillcrest.

Kit must be somewhere nearby, Darby thought, and then she noticed how quietly the dogs approached.

Even though their mouths widened in canine grins, they didn't agitate the cattle.

"Steady," Cade told the dogs, and the two let their alert ears fall as they trailed behind Hula Girl and did their best to take no notice of the cattle.

Cade rode around to Darby's side and nodded.

The movement could have meant "nice job." Cade's compliments were rare. The only thing Darby was sure he didn't mean by the nod was "give me your horse and walk home."

Instead of gushing her thanks, Darby returned his nod and, once more, congratulated her horse.

"You're just as 'cowy' as Jonah thought," she said, and gave Baxter's withers a little massage.

"Not bad," Cade agreed, but just as Darby's spirits soared, he added, "At least it wasn't a full-blown wreck."

In cattlemen's terms, a wreck could be a stampede, a fall from a horse, anything unplanned and disastrous, and even though Cade had said the herd's response to her herding *hadn't* been a wreck, Darby winced.

"You stay relaxed and he'll get the hang of it soon," Cade said. "More practice and you two'll make a team."

"Good," Darby said, but it wasn't Baxter she worried about.

The horse had been bred for cow sense. She hadn't, and she had a lot to learn.

"When you know what you're doing, he'll feel it,"

Cade said. "Baxter's a fast learner."

"I know *he* is," Darby said.

According to her grandfather, Darby was a natural rider, but she was unsettled by her mistakes. They weren't too important here on 'Iolani Ranch, but biting the dust in front of crowded stands at a rodeo was something else.

And that was what she was practicing for: a real rodeo. She'd agreed to compete on Baxter in the *keiki*—Hawaiian for "kids"—ranch rodeo.

"Speaking of learning," she said, "I'd better get back to Sun House and hit the books some more. I have finals *and* a presentation this week."

"Your grades are good." Cade's tone made fun of her fretting.

"So far," she admitted, "but that could change if I flunk anything."

"You won't. You're the girl who loves to read." Cade turned Hula Girl back toward the house, and Darby followed on Baxter.

"Reading plays and novels is fun," she said. "Memorizing algebraic formulas and the capitals of major cities isn't. And oral presentations scare me."

Cade had better not bring up any of her recent adventures like facing a rabid boar or rescuing horses from rising floodwaters. Given a choice between those events and speaking to a class while her hands trembled and her voice shook, she'd pick tusks and tsunamis.

"You're lucky to be earning your diploma by

correspondence," she told Cade.

He shrugged. "I guess so. There didn't seem to be much sense spending my day in a classroom when I already know what I want to be. And training to be a paniolo with Jonah—I'm apprenticed to the best."

Darby nodded, certain Cade *was* learning from a great horseman.

Those who called Jonah "the horse charmer" knew he wasn't only a superior rider and trainer; he could think like a horse.

"Kit and Kimo, too," Cade put in. "They might not have the reputation, but they teach me stuff every day."

Kit Ely was the ranch foreman. A former saddle bronc rodeo rider who'd stopped competing after a broken wrist, he was often mistaken for a Hawaiian. He was really half Shoshone, from Nevada.

Kimo called himself a ranch hand, insisting he was no paniolo because they had to work too hard, but the native Hawaiian, square and solidly built, was an expert horseman.

"What's this presentation?" Cade asked.

"Not sure yet. I'm working with Ann, and our talk is supposed to show off our communication skills."

Ann Potter was Darby's best friend, and they were excited to be working together, since they were both fanatics about getting good grades.

Darby hoped Ann's liveliness would overcome her own shyness. It should. After all, before coming to

Hawaii Darby had rarely spoken up at all. Now she managed to take a stand when she had to, especially if she was speaking up for horses.

Darby knew the presentation would be okay, but it could be a lot better if she was less distracted by the rodeo.

It wasn't much of a problem to Ann. When Megan, Cade, and Darby had invited her to join them so that they could enter as a four-person team in events like doctoring, sorting, and trailer loading, Ann had been excited, but she'd insisted most of her practice hours would have to happen after finals.

And Ann was already an amazing rider. She'd probably be a winner even without practice, Darby thought. Besides, Ann hadn't made the promises Darby had.

When Darby had slipped and told her mother about the rodeo, Ellen had made Darby promise she wouldn't shortchange her studies. Getting good grades was a condition for Darby staying in Hawaii while her mother, Ellen, an actress, filmed a TV series in Tahiti. Ellen had even implied that if Darby seemed to be doing well when she came back from Tahiti on her next break, she'd consider moving to Hawaii for good.

Darby longed to stay on 'Iolani Ranch forever. Her mom, who had grown up here, had wanted nothing more than to leave and head for Hollywood to pursue her acting career.

Darby could hardly believe it. Her first steps

on the soil of 'Iolani Ranch had convinced her that Hawaii had been in her blood all along, just waiting for her to discover it. She might be only part Hawaiian, but she was one hundred percent in love with this island.

Cade walked Hula Girl alongside Baxter and Darby until they reached the gate.

"I'll get it this time," Darby said, and she celebrated silently when Baxter took her close enough to reach the bolt, then sidestepped away to hold it open.

It was Hula Girl who acted up.

The chestnut mare held her head high and pricked her ears, frozen in place despite Cade's urging. The opening in the fence might have been a steel wall for all the attention she paid it.

A breeze ruffled the ends of Darby's ponytail across her cheek, and she shivered at its tickle as Baxter gave a low, worried whinny.

Cade even clucked his tongue for Hula Girl to move, but she wouldn't. Her ears flattened. Her nostrils closed in an expression between fear and aggression, and she ignored her rider's signal.

"What is it?" Darby asked, and the instant Hula Girl turned her attention on Darby, Cade used his legs and hands to drive the mare through the gate.

Darby closed it quickly and caught up with Cade as he kept the mare moving.

"Maybe she caught a whiff of Luna Dancer." Cade shrugged and kept the mare in a controlled jog when she would have gone much faster.

Even as a guess, Cade's explanation didn't ring true. The mare had just seen Luna Dancer playing with the other foals as they herded the cattle past, and she'd merely glanced at him. But now the mare was acting provoked and protective.

Without slowing, Cade stood in his stirrups and scanned the hilltops and gullies.

"The only stallion around is Kanaka Luna. She's used to him," Cade mused. "Else I'd say that's what's got her nerved up."

Luna wasn't the only stallion who'd been on the ranch lately, and she and Cade both knew it.

"It could be Black Lava," Darby said.

She pictured the dangerous black stallion, but Cade snorted. "He's not dumb enough to come back here again."

"You like him." Darby heard her accusing tone just as she realized that was why Cade had answered that way. He'd admired the stallion for a long time, and he didn't want Black Lava to risk a return. After all, Jonah had threatened to shoot him.

The stallion's herd should be living in Crimson Vale, the lush waterfall valley where Cade had once lived. After the tsunami, the wild horses had been herded ashore and eventually relocated to Sky Mountain to keep them away from the tsunami-tainted water.

Cade shook his head, but he didn't look like he had any brainpower left for arguing. Hula Girl moved with mincing steps, and all of Cade's attention was focused on her.

"What if Snowfire drove Black Lava off his territory?" Darby asked, and Cade flashed her a look that clearly instructed her to be quiet.

But it could be—she'd seen Snowfire, the wild white stallion whose herd ranged on Sky Mountain. In the midst of a volcanic eruption, he'd still looked mighty. Muscular and wise, with a long, curly mane, he ruled over Sky Mountain and would not welcome an invading stallion in his territory.

A fight between those two stallions—Snowfire, powerful and smart, against Black Lava's strength and youth—would be like a collision of thunderclouds, complete with bolts of lightning, Darby thought.

When Hula Girl blasted a warning neigh northward, across the pastures, Darby knew whichever horse had lost that battle might have been driven onto 'Iolani Ranch lands whether he wanted to be there or not.

 Chapter Two

Cade might have seen the steer first if he hadn't taken Hula Girl on ahead, making her back up in a straight line, then perform a side pass, forcing her to think of where she was putting her feet, instead of the disturbing scent on the wind.

But it was Baxter who sighted the steer, and jolted Darby from her daydream of wild stallions.

Unlike the red Hereford cattle they'd been herding, this steer's coat was a mix of brown, yellow, and black. But the most distinctive thing about him was a crumpled horn.

The broken ends of the horn stuck up, ragged and discolored with dried blood.

That injury has to hurt, Darby guessed. The

wandering steer was in no mood to be herded. He might have sensed Baxter's inexperience, too, because he struck his cloven hoof at the grass, then lowered his head.

Would he charge? That broken horn hinted he'd done it before.

She wasn't a matador and he wasn't a fighting bull, but Darby was learning that range cattle were not the same animals she'd seen in storybooks and on milk cartons. Some—like this one—could be downright fierce.

Baxter snorted and strained against the reins, trying to lower his own head.

"A face-off is not a great idea, Bax," Darby whispered.

A horse and a steer wouldn't really charge each other, would they? She tried not to think of a Spanish bullring, of sharp horns heaving gaily decorated horses off the ground.

Darby shortened her reins even more, sat hard into her saddle, and made Baxter back away. "He's just showing off," she told the blue roan. "We're not going to fight about it."

Cade's high-pitched whistle blasted into the air, summoning Jack and Jill.

Darby had forgotten all about the cow-wise Australian shepherds, but Cade hadn't.

"Come by," he told the dogs, and they raced clockwise around the steer, bringing him toward Cade until the paniolo signaled them to move the animal to the Upper Sugar Mill pasture.

"Wait," Cade said to Darby, as he sent Hula Girl between the two dogs, right on the steer's heels.

They moved at a lope, right up the hill and through the dense green grasses, about ten times as fast as she and Cade had moved the first bunch.

Darby's heart quit pounding and she laughed with relief. She felt a little embarrassed at the speed with which Cade could do the task without her, but she tried to concentrate on memorizing the many risks that could pop up if you worked with living, thinking creatures. Like cows.

When Cade returned, Hula Girl was prancing and blowing importantly through her nostrils. Obviously the mare wasn't worried anymore.

"Do you think it was that steer—?" Darby asked, and maybe because he let her get only half of it out, Cade didn't exactly answer her question.

"She's okay now," he said, nodding down at his horse, and he was right. Whatever danger Hula Girl had sensed had passed.

As they rode down the mountainside Darby stayed focused on Baxter's every movement. She watched his ears, the angle of his head, and the swishing of his tail. She felt for tension beneath the saddle. Even though Baxter had shown no signs of bucking today, she reminded herself that his nickname was *Buckin'* Baxter.

According to Jonah, a horse couldn't buck if he was moving forward with his head up, so Darby kept her reins in straight lines to the snaffle rings in order to keep the thin metal bars in place, assuring the gelding that she was paying attention.

When the path widened, she moved Baxter forward so that she could talk to Cade. "Jack and Jill really handled that cow."

"Jonah's an amazing trainer. He's got all the dogs thinking they're caretakers."

Darby raised her eyebrows, and Cade went on.

"They don't take any nonsense from cattle, but they don't run them or bark a lot. A scared cow uses more calories and runs off fat."

"Because they earn their keep, uh, by the pound, right?" Darby said.

Cade nodded, but his brown eyes met Darby's, checking to see whether she understood.

"I get it," she told him. "I know they're sold for meat. Kimo said each cow's worth about a thousand dollars."

Cade nodded once more, but he didn't look satisfied.

Cade drove her crazy when he expected her to read his mind, but if she demanded he tell her what was wrong, he'd clam up and quit talking altogether.

She knew Jonah's cattle business barely broke even. She knew the market for beef that was grass fed—rather than stuffed with grain and chemicals—was growing, but slowly. She also knew the ranch lived by its horses. Was that what Cade was getting at?

"And Jonah wants us to use the *keiki* ranch rodeo to show off the horses, to bring in more money," Darby said.

"Well, uh, yeah."

"Because the rodeo attracts tourists and horse people," Darby added. She wished she hadn't ended the sentence with a sigh. Just because she was attached to every animal on the ranch didn't mean she didn't understand business.

As Darby stroked Baxter's neck, his jog turned lighter. He liked to be appreciated and he liked her touch.

Guilt panged through her chest, leaving an ache. Baxter, Hula Girl, and Conch were the horses Jonah hoped to sell. Practicing on Baxter made her like him more—but also made him more salable.

"Here's the thing," Cade blurted. He looked straight ahead, through Hula Girl's ears, instead of facing Darby. "I know you didn't mean to, but runnin' Baxter after cattle and yelling at 'em—that runs off fat, too."

Darby's face went hot.

Get back! she'd whooped at the cattle, while she'd swung her arm around. Then she'd chased after the calf, which was probably okay, but she'd swung Baxter around hard and galloped crazily back at them.

So that was what Cade had been trying to tell her

by talking about the dogs.

This Hawaiian habit of telling stories to make a point didn't always get through to her mainland brain.

"Sorry," Darby said, and Cade must have felt embarrassed, too, because he not only started a conversation, he changed the subject.

"So, uh. It was really nice of Kimo to repair Manny's old truck for Mom," he said.

"Kimo's the best," she agreed, adding to herself that Cade's mom, Dee, was lucky that everyone around her was willing to forget she'd been a bad mother, and give her a second chance.

"I want to repay him, and I was thinking . . ." Cade's face brightened. "It wouldn't be a big deal, but I bet he'd like Mom's coco-mac cookies. Coconut and macadamia nuts . . ." He drew the words out and closed his eyes as if he tasted one. "She made them every Friday before . . . you know."

Darby was pretty sure she *did* know. Dee had made them before she hooked up with Manny, the stepfather who'd forced Cade to squeeze into ancient burial caves in the pali, the sea cliffs, in search of treasure. Of course, it was illegal and scary—there were skeletons in there—but Manny had beaten Cade when he resisted.

Once Jonah found out what Manny was up to, he had taken Cade in. Cade had been Jonah's foster—or *hanai'd*, in Hawaiian—son ever since.

Now that Manny was in jail, Cade was thinking about returning to live with his mother in their ramshackle house in Crimson Vale.

I'm just settling in, Darby thought. *I don't want Cade and the horses going away!*

"Well, the truck's running, anyway," he said, "so Honi's going home."

"Cool!" Darby said, and she couldn't help giving a little bounce in the saddle. "Now Hoku can come home to her corral!"

Cade laughed, so Darby knew he understood, and she didn't have to rush to explain that while she thought Dee's white pony was sweet, Honi's illness had been the reason Hoku had been exiled from her own corral to the pastures below.

As Sun House, the main ranch house, came into view, Darby felt a cozy sense of home. She and Jonah lived downstairs, and her friend Megan shared the upstairs apartment with her mom, the ranch manager who'd asked Darby to call her Aunty Cathy.

One uphill trail would take Darby back to the house, to her room, to studying, but they were riding past the broodmare pasture, and Darby couldn't help looking for her horse.

The filly was easy to pick out. She gleamed redgold in the late-afternoon sunlight and she didn't look like a Quarter Horse. She was a mustang from the high desert of Nevada.

Hoku lifted her head and looked across the grass,

past the other horses, straight at Darby.

"I've got to—"

"I can pony Baxter the rest of the way back," Cade offered before she finished.

"Would you? Thanks. And thanks for not reminding me about studying."

"Books'll wait. She might not," Cade said.

Darby loosely knotted her reins and handed Cade the free end of Baxter's neck rope before she dismounted.

She burst into a jog, headed toward Hoku. The young mustang's ears lifted. Arching her neck, she set off, trotting to meet the girl she trusted.

"Hoku." Darby sang the name, and her heart soared along with her voice. The filly had been just a little standoffish lately, and Darby didn't know if Hoku resented being displaced from her corral or if she'd decided her natural place was among horses, not humans. But now it didn't matter. Hoku stopped right in front of Darby. The filly dusted her lips over Darby's ponytail, doing it so lightly, it gave her goose bumps. Darby tried not to shiver as the horse flared her nostrils and bumped her nose against Darby's shoulder.

Jonah would say Hoku was exerting her dominance, but he couldn't see the gentleness in Hoku's eyes.

"There's my girl." Darby stroked Hoku's neck, but her touch must have been too light, because Hoku's skin shivered and she tossed her head. Darby parted the flaxen forelock covering the mustang's eyes and said, "I've missed you."

Hoku's heart would probably always long to run free, but right this minute, the filly seemed content to be half-tame.

"Guess what?" she asked. "Soon you'll be back in your own corral. Home, sweet home."

Hoku looked satisfied by that revelation, and even though Darby wasn't sure the filly understood, she wondered if her horse's memories of the open range were fading. She felt guilty for robbing the mustang of her wildness.

"Isn't that just like a human?" she asked Hoku. People spotted something wild and beautiful—like a mustang—whose untamed nature thrilled them, and then set about subduing the spirit that had made it so magnificent.

"Would you walk me partway home if I apologized for my species?" Darby asked.

Together they walked in lazy steps, Darby leading her horse by a strand of mane. They were enjoying a breeze that couldn't decide if it should cool down for the approaching evening, when Hoku jerked away.

Darby was about to apologize when she realized Hoku hadn't been pulling away from her. Something on the ridge had caught the filly's attention. With her head flung high and her entire body tensed, Hoku focused on . . . what?

Darby stood almost cheek to cheek with her horse,

lining up her gaze with Hoku's.

There! Against the copper sky, she made out the silhouette of a horse. Two horses. Just then Black Lava and his herd spilled over the ridgetop.

Hula Girl had been right. There *was* a stallion nearby.

No—there were two of them.

Snowfire was a white crest on the dark wave of horses, and as soon as the mares had widened the gap between themselves and the pale stallion, Black Lava wheeled to face him.

 Chapter Three

Snowfire, broad and powerful, looked even more mythical than Darby remembered. He stopped suddenly, as if this were his first sight of the ranch below.

But if the white stallion was puzzled by his surroundings, Black Lava knew exactly where he was. He traversed the hillside on a crooked path and then paused with his head lowered.

Both stallions wore dark patches of sweat, as if this chase had gone on for hours, and Snowfire gave a sharp squeal at his out-of-reach foe.

The wild horses strutted with chins tucked and manes waving.

Black Lava's answering cry, high-pitched and taunting, carried down the slope. Though his mares were uninterested, just stopping to grab a few mouthfuls of grass as they walked down the hillside away from him, Hoku was fascinated.

When another neigh, deeper and raspier, rang out, Darby knew it was Kanaka Luna. She heard the stallion's hooves thunder up and down the length of his compound fence, warning the others away. But Darby and Hoku didn't look, and neither did the wild stallions. They both tested the steep footing, deciding what to do next.

Black Lava's ears flattened. Snowfire reared, keeping his balance above the black stallion, ignoring his threat.

Something must have told Black Lava that Snowfire wouldn't follow, so the black stallion leaped from the ridge and navigated the rocky trail down to the pasture, where his herd waited.

Whether he was answering the fenced-in Luna or taunting Black Lava, Darby couldn't tell, but Snowfire gave a final scream of defiance.

For an instant the white stallion stood still. Proud and mysterious, he was every bit Moho, the island god of steam. And just as quickly as steam, he vanished.

Hoku didn't move. She stared, unblinking, at the spot where Snowfire had been. Finally she gave a snort and shook her head, as if clearing away his image.

"I know," Darby agreed. "Wow."

It took Darby a second to realize why Luna was still neighing and patrolling his fence at a gallop.

Black Lava remained on Luna's land, within sight of Luna's mares. Black Lava had had the audacity to bring his herd here instead of going home to Crimson Vale. But why? And where was the rest of the herd?

While Black Lava picked his way down the trail, Darby counted one sleek bay, a chestnut, a black, and a dun, plus one foal in the herd. She'd noticed this foal, ink black and tiny, before. She'd always thought of him as the youngest of Black Lava's sons, but now he seemed to be the *only* one.

Could Black Lava's herd have dwindled to just four mares and this colt?

She felt sorry for him, though he sure didn't look pitiful. As the trail grew less steep, he descended faster.

And suddenly, Darby knew why Black Lava had come down from Sky Mountain to the ranch instead of returning to Crimson Vale. He needed more mares, and he knew where to find them.

Panic grabbed Darby's chest. She couldn't let this happen. Black Lava could strike and be gone before anyone paid attention to Luna's screams.

Upon reaching the bottom of the trail, Black Lava sprinted into a breakneck gallop and easily cleared the fence of the broodmare pasture.

Darby had been close to the wild stallion before and felt this same sense of awe. Despite the danger he was beautiful, with his black mane swirling around him like a storm cloud. If he just stayed away from Hoku . . .

For a moment, the broodmares stared in bewilderment at the wild stallion, but then they were all moving together, blocking the dark intruder's view of their foals.

Hoku's ears stood straight up. She stayed beside Darby, not joining the knot of protective mares. Still, there could be no question that the sorrel was on alert.

But Black Lava hadn't noticed Hoku, and the only other mare apart from the others was Tango, Megan's pink roan mare.

The black stallion was after her.

No! Darby thought as the stallion raced in Tango's direction. The mare burst into a gallop, but Black Lava was right behind her, head lowered. He herded her to the fence, urging her to leap toward freedom. But Tango swerved away and hid herself amid the herd of broodmares and foals.

As if he'd suddenly lost interest in the chase, Black Lava careened off course. In a floating trot that looked almost slow-motion, he came at them, and Darby realized she'd been wrong.

Of course Black Lava had noticed Hoku. He just wasn't up for a fight.

After his dash down the mountain and his pursuit of Tango, the mustang's black coat was banded with lather, and he was breathing hard.

Hoku flattened her ears and faced him, and in that instant Darby saw she needn't have worried about

Hoku's wild instincts deserting her. The filly bumped Darby out of the way, just as a mother would her foal.

Tufts of earth and grass flew up from Hoku's hooves as the filly charged Black Lava.

She's protecting me, Darby thought in amazement. She pressed both hands over her mouth, afraid she might shout a warning. Distracting Hoku now could be fatal.

The black stallion and golden filly came together like horses in a jousting match. Their shoulders brushed as they rushed past each other, then wheeled for a second encounter.

Darby's heart pounded. She didn't want to look, but she couldn't turn away, because this time Hoku's slashing teeth and striking hooves missed the stallion by only inches.

Black Lava had no intention of fighting a slender female half his size. He backed up a few steps, then reared, flashing a feathered foreleg out at an awkward angle.

Cuts marked his legs and haunches. Red rips ran across his ebony neck.

From Snowfire? Darby hoped Black Lava was weary from that clash.

Arms wrapped around herself, Darby rocked forward and back. The stallion clearly didn't want this battle. Why didn't he simply go away?

Black Lava turned abruptly. With a backward glance at the group of broodmares he hadn't stolen, the stallion broke into a run, aimed for the white fence, and sailed over it.

His herd reassembled behind him and ran west, away from 'Iolani Ranch, toward the rain forest.

Hot and wet, her sorrel body steaming from nerves and exertion, Hoku returned to Darby.

"You're okay," she croaked to her horse.

They stood together, unified by relief, love, and the adrenaline surging through their veins.

As Hoku's breathing slowed, so did Darby's, and she began to wonder about Black Lava. He and his herd had been driven up the mountain by the Wildlife Conservancy so they wouldn't drink the contaminated water of Crimson Vale.

What if Black Lava had decided he knew best, and he'd followed the scents of sea spray and red lehua flowers, so abundant in Crimson Vale, toward home?

When he was rested, would Black Lava return for 'Iolani mares to replenish his herd?

The ranch came first, Cade had reminded her today. And whether that meant not harassing cows with her inexperience, not regretting the sale of beloved horses, or not protecting a wild stallion who'd had his "last chance" several times over, Darby knew she had to tell Jonah what had happened.

"Gotta go, girl," Darby told Hoku.

She gave the filly's shoulder a loud pat and took off. She ran across the pasture, climbed over the fence instead of taking extra time to open and close the gate, and then raced for the trail up to Sun House.

Darby had almost reached the top of the path when a *pueo* swooped out of the sky, dropping so low she heard feathers rustle. She'd seen Hawaiian owls during daylight plenty of times, but never like this.

Light reflected off the inside of pale, fanning wings as the owl looked down at her. It hovered so close she saw the widow's peak of feathers above lemon-drop eyes in a round face. And then it was dropping, talons extended.

Darby ducked and crossed her arms over her head.

What had gotten into him? Owls were supposed to be her family's *'aumakua*, but this was no shielding ancestor. This was one insane bird.

Finally the tumult of wings stopped, and when Darby opened her eyes just a crack to look around, the owl was gone.

She resumed her run.

Almost there, she thought, placing her boots as carefully and quickly as she could. *Almost home.*

All the while, Hoku's whinny echoed behind her, but there'd be time to make it up to her filly later.

Panting and breathless, Darby didn't see anyone around when she reached the level ground of the ranch yard. She turned toward Sun House, hurried inside, and plopped down on the bench by the front door to yank off her riding boots.

She smelled curry simmering in the kitchen, but heard none of the cooking sounds she expected this close to dinnertime.

Lining her own scuffed boots up with the others gave Darby a few seconds to think, but her mind was spinning. As she crossed the dim living room and headed for the lanai, she still wasn't sure what she should say.

Two men and one woman stood talking out there.

Her grandfather, Jonah Kealoha, with his thick black mustache and pressed blue shirt tucked into khaki pants, paced beside the table on the lanai. He stayed silent, but something about the contained energy of his steps made Darby sure he was full of opinions. As she watched, Jonah stopped and crossed his arms, listening to Kit and Aunty Cathy, who were both seated at the table.

Darby's steps slowed when she saw Kit. The ranch foreman usually kept to himself.

"What's wrong?" Jonah saw her before the others, but they turned at her grandfather's tone of voice.

"We got the cattle to Upper Sugar Mills," Darby started.

"Yeah. Cade reported in. What else?" Jonah asked.

"Snowfire and Black Lava were both—"

"—here?" Jonah finished.

Darby nodded as her grandfather smacked one fist into the cup of his other hand.

"Snowfire was just chasing Black Lava, though," Darby said. "Like, getting him off his territory, I think."

Aunty Cathy leaned her elbow on the table, then her cheek against her hand. From beneath her bangs her eyes narrowed, as they did when she was making calculations.

"We're a long way from Sky Mountain," Aunty Cathy observed.

"I know, but I don't know why else . . ." Darby shook her head, then interrupted herself. "There *are* mares missing from Black Lava's herd, but he's probably just headed for home. I thought I should tell you he was here, though . . ." Darby's words trailed off as she struggled for breath.

"Did he go for the mares?" Jonah asked.

Darby hesitated. She placed a hand on her chest, but Jonah wasn't fooled. He didn't believe she was trying to catch her breath. He knew she was stalling, trying to decide how much she should say about the stallion's actions.

"Speak up," Jonah snapped.

The next time, Black Lava might be fresh and finished with battling Snowfire. The next time, Hoku might not scare him off. The next time, he might goad the broodmares into a stampede through the wooden fence and drive them to his hidden realm in Crimson Vale.

"He came over the fence and chased Tango," Darby admitted.

"The broodmares faced him down?" Kit asked.

Darby nodded.

"And Hoku?" Aunty Cathy asked.

All over again, Darby saw her filly's flashing teeth and sorrel satin ears flattened into her mane.

"She stood up to him," Darby said.

"But you're all right?" Aunty Cathy bolted to her feet and reached out to touch Darby's disheveled ponytail.

"I'm fine," Darby said. "And Hoku is, too."

"Tomboy mare, that one." Jonah winked, then reconsidered. "Someday a stallion's not gonna back down. Then she'll get herself hurt."

Darby swallowed hard and nodded. It was one of the thoughts that had driven her away from Hoku and up to the house. Still, she hated having Jonah, an expert, confirm her fear.

She pretended to fuss with her ponytail, smoothing the strands Hoku had nuzzled loose. But Darby didn't care about her hair. She felt sick as she thought of a powerful stallion turning his fury on Hoku.

Aunty Cathy noticed Darby's fidgeting.

"Mares don't always get the worst of it," she said. "Most lead range stallions have scars from where they've been kicked by mares."

"Black Lava had a lot of injuries," Darby recalled,

picturing the stallion. "He had some bleeding cuts and a gash on his neck, plus the old scars on his chest."

"Been fightin' Snowfire," Kit said.

When Aunty Cathy and Jonah nodded, Darby made the suggestion that had been brewing in her mind.

"That's why—besides the fact that we don't want him around here—I was thinking we should help Black Lava and his herd get back to Crimson Vale."

"Wild stallion like him should be able to find his way home, even if"—Jonah held his hand up when Darby began to interrupt—"the tsunami and earthquake have changed things. And I'll tell you, Darby Leilani, the black horse is better off steering clear of me. If I go looking for him again, it's the last time."

Darby was scared for Black Lava until Jonah rubbed the back of his neck and sighed. That took the venom out of his threat.

"So, how did Baxter do with the cattle?" Aunty Cathy asked. "We were talking about the rodeo when you came in."

"Really well," Darby said. "He's got the instincts to go after cows, but both of us need some work."

"We just got the list of events," Kit said, tapping a piece of paper. "And Kimo thinks Baxter'll do best in the ranch ones."

"Like sorting and doctoring cattle, and the trailer-loading race," Aunty Cathy said. "And since Kimo's ridden him the most and says those events are the most like what Baxter's already been doing—"

"I wish Kimo wasn't too old to ride him," Darby said. Kimo was only in his twenties, but the *keiki* rodeo allowed no contestants over eighteen.

"He and Jonah have volunteered to help as pickup riders," Kit said, smiling.

Darby would bet his grin reflected the good times he'd had rodeoing, because bull and bronc riders were often helped off their bucking mounts, or out of the arena by pickup riders.

"Conch, Baxter, Hula Girl, and Lady Wong," Jonah said, ticking the names off on his fingers as he said them.

"What about them?" Darby asked.

"They'll show the best and bring in the best prices."

"Lady Wong?" Darby didn't want to sell any of the horses, but this was the first time she'd heard her grandfather mention selling the gray Thoroughbred.

"Showin' the quality of our broodmares," Jonah said.

"But she's not for sale," Kit put in.

I wish Baxter weren't, Darby thought.

"Don't you think that people who see Kimo on Cash will want to come ride the cremellos?" Aunty Cathy added, and Darby nodded her agreement.

Cash was a trim, mannerly horse, one of the

cremellos Jonah had accepted from his sister, Darby's aunt Babe, who owned Sugar Sands Cove Resort. Babe Borden had given her brother the cremellos with the understanding that he'd allow her guests to come ride them on 'Iolani Ranch.

Darby sighed, glad Aunty Cathy hadn't meant Cash was for sale. Of course she hadn't. She was the one who'd come up with the idea to make a little extra money doing dude rides with the cremellos.

"It will be good advertising for both 'Iolani Ranch and the resort," Aunty Cathy said.

By the way she said it, Darby could tell she wanted a little backup.

"It will," Darby agreed, and Aunty Cathy smiled at the same time Jonah groaned.

He hated words like *advertising* and *public relations*. He wasn't too fond of *budget*, either, and he left that for the ranch manager, Aunty Cathy, to worry about.

"No complaining," Aunty Cathy said. "You're the one who came up with the idea to ride Kanaka Luna."

And it was a good idea, Darby thought. When they saw Luna, people would want to breed their mares to him or buy his offspring. The stallion was the undisputed king of 'Iolani Ranch—beautiful, athletic, and good-tempered (most of the time). Showing him off made good business sense. She didn't see any reason to mention how upset he'd been by Black Lava.

The phone rang, and Aunty Cathy headed for the kitchen to answer it, rubbing Darby's back with brisk affection as she passed.

Darby's mind darted between thoughts of the rodeo and Black Lava. What if the stallion's wounds got infected? What if he'd lost too much blood?

Jonah was staring off the lanai, so Darby took the chance to ask Kit a quiet question. "Don't you think we should check on Black Lava?"

Kit took his time answering, but that was no surprise. Darby had decided cowboys the world over were the same about slow, careful talking, at least the ones she'd met.

"Seems like the Nature Conservancy wants the herd away from that Crimson Vale water."

"But you're a wild horse expert," Darby insisted.

"Not like them," Kit said. "I finished high school, is all."

"You grew up with wild horses," Darby said.

Jonah's jaw was set hard. His mouth barely opened when he said, "He told you he's no expert. You grew up in a house with running water. You call yourself a plumber?"

Darby looked down at the wood boards of the lanai and shook her head.

Jonah had been this sarcastic and mean when she'd first moved to Moku Lio Hihiu, hadn't he? Why had she forgotten how to take it? More important, what had made him relapse?

"Could I get Cade to go with me to check on them?" Darby asked Jonah.

Jonah leaned back against the rail of the lanai, studying Darby.

"He puko'a ku noka moana," he said.

If there was anything more frustrating than being mocked in a language you didn't speak, Darby didn't know what it was. But Jonah usually couldn't resist telling the story behind his sayings, so she waited patiently.

"A large rock standing in the sea," Jonah explained, but his translation made it no clearer.

"I'm just looking for a solution to this problem," she said.

"The only problem," Jonah said, "is that black horse keeps showin' up where he's not wanted."

"I'll be okay if Cade comes with me." Darby pretended she hadn't heard her grandfather.

"Cade's busy packin' Honi off to Dee's place. Isn't that what you want? So Miss Crazy Horse can come back up here?"

"Yes," Darby said, then studied the floorboards again.

Jonah's bad moods were contagious. She must not be the only one who thought so, because Kit was edging off the lanai, toward the door.

"I could ride after them by myself." Darby was only trying to give Kit some cover, but it didn't work.

"No, you couldn't," Jonah told her.

"On Navigator," Darby added.

Just then Aunty Cathy returned, and Jonah gestured toward Darby.

"Riding out into the middle of a wild herd all by herself tonight. How's that sound?"

"That's not what I said." Darby spoke quietly. "I can't go tonight. Besides studying, I . . . well, since Honi's well and going back to live with Dee, I can bring Hoku up to her own corral."

"About *that*," Aunty Cathy said. Her smile was apologetic as she gestured toward the kitchen phone. "Our caller was Cricket."

Kit stopped moving toward the front door. He looked a little confused. Since Cricket was his girlfriend, he probably wondered why she hadn't phoned the foreman's house, or at least asked for him.

"She wanted to talk to me and have me talk to Jonah, but since you're all here, I'll tell you together.

"Cricket has to make room for more sick horses at the Hapuna Animal Rescue barn. Since Medusa is 'maintaining her good health'"—Aunty Cathy made quotation marks in the air, so they'd know she was repeating exactly what Cricket had said—"Cricket wants to get Medusa away from the other, possibly sick, horses. If she's exposed to something she has no immunities against, because she's wild, it could hit her pretty hard."

Medusa was the first steeldust Darby had ever

seen. Dove gray all over, she was flecked with black and white and named for her long, curly black mane and tail.

She'd been Black Lava's lead mare until the tsunami. Fear and injuries from sharp rocks had separated her from her herd, and for the last couple of weeks she'd been in quarantine at the rescue barn.

"Makes sense," Kit said.

Darby heard his hesitation, even though he'd filled out the paperwork to adopt the wild mare.

"So," Aunty Cathy said to Jonah and Kit, "Cricket wants to know if we can take her here. Now."

Kit's application to adopt Medusa must have been approved. Instead of celebrating, though, he looked tense.

It was so quiet Darby heard Hoku neighing from the broodmare pasture.

Darby suddenly knew why it was so quiet, and why Kit had just glanced at her.

Cricket wants to know if we can take her here. Now.

The only corral strong enough to hold a wild horse was Hoku's. If Medusa moved in, it meant Hoku had to stay in the pasture down below. Her training would be put off even longer.

Hoku's lonely whinny came again, and when Darby looked at Kit, his expression had changed.

"Well?" Aunty Cathy asked.

"Course, it's up to the boss," Kit told her.

Darby's heart plummeted. Kit would go along with

whatever Jonah decreed, but her grandfather would probably vote to keep his foreman happy. And anyone on the island could see that Kit was working hard not to show his excitement.

 Chapter Four

Jonah didn't turn around. He leaned his forearms on the rail of the lanai and stared at the rolling ranch lands.

"Black Lava could be gone for good," Jonah mused. "And he might not notice us bringin' his lead mare in here, even if he stays around."

A wild turkey called from somewhere. Jonah patted the rail with both hands, then turned to look at Darby.

"You decide," he said.

"Why me?"

"Who better? It's your horse gettin' wilder by the day."

"But it's your ranch," Darby pointed out.

"What's the difference between one *pupule* mare and another?" Jonah asked, but he kept talking and gesturing at the grounds below. "Goat over here. Pig over there. Dude horses carrying tourists who'll cut trails into every acre of grass. Pretty soon I won't even recognize this place!"

Darby, Kit, and Aunty Cathy stood frozen at Jonah's outburst.

"Excuse me," he said, brushing past Darby as he turned to leave the lanai.

"I'm sorry," Darby called after him.

Her grandfather didn't answer, and when she turned back to Aunty Cathy and Kit, she saw they both looked somber, but not surprised. Had the swooping *pueo* been a warning of bad things to come? Medusa moving into Hoku's corral. Jonah's temper. And what else? Wasn't misfortune supposed to come in sets of three?

And then it hit her. He might not mean he wouldn't recognize the ranch because it was changing. He could be talking about his eyesight.

Jonah had confessed to Darby and her mother that he had a condition that had slowly been robbing him of his vision.

"Did he mean . . . ?" Darby caught her breath. Though she was pretty sure Aunty Cathy knew about Jonah's eyes, what about Kit?

She didn't have to ask.

"Yeah, I know. Have since he hired me," Kit told

her. "Cade doesn't know." Kit's tone was both caution-ing and harsh, but there was something touching in it, too.

"I won't tell," Darby promised. And then some-thing made her look at Aunty Cathy.

Head bent, she was buttoning the open collar of her sleeveless shirt as high as it would go. Then she put her hands on her hips and regarded Darby.

"Jonah doesn't want Cade's decision on whether to stay here or go home to be influenced by pity," Aunty Cathy said. "But I think this"—she gestured to the lanai as if the scene were still taking place—"was more about the concessions we're making to the economy."

"The tourist rides?" Darby asked, and Aunty Cathy nodded.

"Even though he doesn't act like it, he doesn't want to make either of you unhappy."

"What would you do with Medusa if she couldn't come here?" Darby asked Kit.

The foreman looked down at the black Stetson he'd been holding all along. He turned it in his hands as if he were studying the flare of its brim, then slowly shook his head.

"Don't know, but the boss has a point. My mare might bring Black Lava back, and it'll be no small thing if he steals a good Quarter Horse mare or two while he's around."

"We could isolate her in the round corral," Aunty Cathy suggested, "and put Hoku back in hers, but the racket would be pretty intense. Really, I don't think those two should be within earshot of each other, but it's a solution."

She raised her eyebrows as she looked at Darby.

"Nope," Kit said. He swallowed, and Darby got the feeling the cowboy had rarely talked so much in a single day. "Even if that corral would hold her, it's too far away. I want her next to me, so that if that black stud shows up I can take care of things."

Darby remembered the first time she'd seen Black Lava trespass on the ranch. She'd noticed Kit and Jonah studying a hoofprint together and wondered why, since Jonah was the one who'd marked the stallion's hoof and would recognize it.

Kit had never let on that anything was wrong with Jonah's eyes, and she'd bet he never would.

Darby took a deep breath and held it until it hurt.

There's such a thing as loyalty, she scolded herself. And right now loyalty to her family, especially to her grandfather, and those who were faithful to him, like Kit, was more important than loyalty to her horse.

After all, it was Jonah who'd paid Hoku's way across the Pacific Ocean to Hawaii. Jonah had handed her a world of horses and all but promised her this ranch.

"Hoku's okay where she is, for now," Darby blurted before she could change her mind. "Go ahead and tell Cricket she can bring Medusa here."

Darby felt as though she'd stepped out of her own

body and joined Kit and Aunty Cathy in staring at her in shocked surprise.

"That's my vote," she snapped, when they kept gawking at her. "It's no crime to be mature, yeah?"

She was embarrassed by her outburst until she saw Aunty Cathy smother a laugh.

There was nothing funny about this.

Darby missed having Hoku so close she could hear her hoofbeats through her bedroom window. She missed hand-feeding her hay. She wanted to continue the filly's training, because they'd already come so close to striking a balance. Hoku had been a one-girl horse, wild to everyone except Darby, but that bond could vanish. What if that was the third stroke of misfortune?

Darby heard steps coming down from the upstairs apartment. They had to belong to Megan. Too bad her unofficial big sis hadn't seen her self-sacrifice, because Megan thought Darby was just a little too indulgent when it came to Hoku.

"Won't be forever." Kit got the words out, but he addressed them to his hat.

"I know," she said.

"If you want, I'll work with you 'n' Hoku. Every chance I get."

The blush under Kit's tanned skin darkened from pink to rose to bandanna red, but he forced himself to go on. "She'll be saddle gentle in no time. If you want."

"I do," she said.

With a nod, Kit bolted off the lanai and into the house. They heard his boots clomping fast.

"He's a good guy," Aunty Cathy said. "You won't be sorry, Darby."

I'm already sorry, she thought.

Just then Megan, her long cherry Coke–colored hair swinging around her cheeks, popped out onto the lanai.

"What's up with Kit?" she asked. "When he passed me he was mumbling something about being bashful as an old maid skinning a skunk. Could that be right?"

Aunty Cathy had agreed to do kitchen cleanup alone during finals week, so Darby's conscience only let her pause for a moment when Megan tried to get her to watch TV before she settled down to study.

"We have dead day tomorrow," Megan said. "No classes, just a study day."

"I know," Darby said.

"The day after that there's P.E., and that final's going to be a piece of cake. I kind of don't like having my easy day first," Megan said. "I'd rather have it last."

"My Ecology final's on the same day as P.E.," Darby said. "And I've got to memorize lots of stuff."

Darby mentally reviewed her finals schedule. Ecology and Sports P.E. came first, then Creative Writing and Algebra, and finally English and History.

"I don't think I have an easy day all week," she said.

"Poor Darby," Megan said. "Then I'll let you go study, but first I have to tell you what I saw over at the rodeo grounds." Megan clicked the remote to mute the TV, flung her long legs over the arm of the couch, and lay back to describe the rodeo fairgrounds she'd checked out with her mom while Darby and Cade herded cattle.

"The arena's a big rectangle, with stands for the audience on the long sides, chutes for holding calves and steers until they're released for, you know, calf roping and stuff, and the other end has a big gate that swings wide, and you wait there until your time starts for barrel racing and . . . It's just going to be so awesome!" Megan jumped up, unable to contain her enthusiasm.

"Which horses are you riding?" Darby asked.

"Conch, I think. Maybe Lady Wong." She shrugged. "I'll know better when I see the list of events."

"Kit has one," Darby told her, and tried not to think of the scene on the lanai and Jonah's quiet mood during dinner.

"Great! Maybe I'll walk down to the bunkhouse and take a look at it."

"Cade left to drive Honi home," Darby pointed out, since he and Kit shared the bunkhouse.

"Like I care." Megan rolled her eyes in exasperation, then turned her full attention on Darby. "Wait, so, hey! How did Buckin' Baxter treat you?"

"No bucking, at least."

"And . . ." Megan rolled one hand through the air, coaxing Darby to tell her more.

So she did, and enjoyed every word.

For most of her life Darby had been an only child. Since her parents' divorce and her dad's remarriage, she'd had younger siblings, but that wasn't the same as having a big sister.

Megan was fifteen, very social, a skilled athlete, and free with her advice. Darby knew Megan Kato was the closest thing she'd ever have to a sister, and she loved their easy friendship.

Megan was an only child, too. But she'd had it far worse than Darby. She hadn't lost her paniolo dad to divorce: He'd died in a riding accident.

Darby sighed, and her gaze wandered to the lanai and the mountains beyond. Dark violet with luminous purple edges, they rolled out to Sky Mountain.

Black Lava was out there somewhere with his four mares and a single black colt. Would he find another way home or was he hiding nearby, maybe at the fold at the end of the road?

Had he left Sky Mountain because he was a jungle horse? Or had Snowfire chased him the many miles to 'Iolani Ranch?

Darby hadn't noticed a scratch on Snowfire, but she remembered Black Lava's wounds. Wild horses had no natural predators, but that didn't mean the black stallion was safe. The slashes on his neck were probably from Snowfire's teeth, and they could get infected.

Darby was wondering why she couldn't stop thinking about that when a pall of heat fell over her. She saw Black Lava on his side on the ground. In feverish protest against his weakness, his legs thrashed.

No weird stuff, Darby told herself. She shook the image from her head. Reading the feelings of a horse standing right in front of her was one thing. Picturing Black Lava like that was just plain morbid.

Had she subconsciously noticed something? And the something had evoked a warning. That had to be it.

I'll go out there to check on them, she decided, *even if I have to go alone.*

"I'd better hit the books," she said suddenly.

Megan still stood before the TV, watching the soundless images of a car chase.

"You're guilting me into it." Megan yawned. "I'd better look over the kinesiology handout Ms. Day gave us."

Ms. Day taught P.E. and English, and she often based her tests on handouts she'd distributed weeks earlier.

"I almost forgot about that," Darby said as Megan turned off the TV.

"Have fun," Megan sang, and then left for her upstairs apartment.

* * *

Darby hurried through her shower, pulled on cotton boxers and a fresh T-shirt, then climbed into bed with her textbooks.

She got out Miss Day's handout along with the stuff for Ecology, then let herself be sidetracked into thinking about her capital-cities test for History. That might be her hardest final.

Luckily, she'd learned some tricks with note cards, color coding, and listing from last year's study-skills teacher. That made memorization easier, and Darby worked for almost two hours without getting sleepy.

It was a little late to call Ann, but time was running out. If they took two days to decide on their presentation topic, they'd only have one day for practice. Darby wanted to end the year with a report card that would stun her mother into believing her daughter wasn't distracted by horses and ranch life, so there was no reason for them to ever leave Moku Lio Hihiu.

She switched off her bedside light and settled under the covers. A minute later she kicked them off.

The night was hot and still. No breeze brought scents of green grass, red dirt, and flowers. No yaps from the dogs or hoofbeats from the horses. No comforting nicker from Hoku, and her longing neighs had stopped, too.

Was she all right out there in the pasture? Was she still there, or had Black Lava come back and stolen her away?

From down the hall came the sound of flipping

pages. Jonah was right where he should be, not staring over the darkened ranch as he sometimes did.

The sound should have been comforting, but Jonah must be going through the papers to register them for the *keiki* rodeo.

How would she do in front of every rider on the island?

Knock it off, she told herself, then snapped the light back on and reached for her diary. She turned to its unlined pages and began drawing horses.

Of course I'm drawing horses. She smiled as her pencil flew over the paper. *They're the only things I can draw!*

She sketched Black Lava's mares. As she worked on the bay mare's legs—hind legs were always the hardest!—she remembered that Tutu had said some people thought they were descendants of the French Camargue marsh horses.

Others thought their bloodlines went back to the Spanish barbs, so she gave one of the mares a more Arab-looking head.

Darby had looked up pictures of the French horses on the Internet in the ranch office. The powerful white horses were supposed to be related to equines from prehistoric times.

Darby shivered. Snowfire looked exactly like a French Camargue.

Almost holding her breath, she drew the white stallion. She gave him broad hooves for walking on the beach and scaling cliffs. She added silky hair to protect him from whipping snow flurries on Sky Mountain, and large, intelligent eyes that could see from the hills to the sea.

At last she tucked her diary away, turned over on one side, and dreamed of horses.

Chapter Five

Megan, Darby, and Cade were waiting outside Sun House when Cricket arrived in her beat-up Jeep, pulling an open horse trailer.

The girls had been finishing breakfast when they'd heard Medusa's neighs.

Fighting the trailer and overwhelmed by the bewildering experience of moving without running, Medusa screamed at the humans who'd caused her confinement.

Kit appeared farther down the road leading into the ranch yard and motioned with both hands, telling Cricket to keep driving until she reached Hoku's corral.

It almost worked.

Darby and Megan jogged behind the trailer until Cricket came to a stop just before she reached the tack shed.

Darby had to admit the horse was magnificent in her fiery steeldust beauty, but her heart ached for the mare. A leader of her own kind, the horse used fury to hide her fear. Darby could see why Cricket was eager to end the mare's imprisonment.

"The ride really freaked her out," Megan sympathized. As Cricket turned off the Jeep, got out, and closed the door softly behind her, Megan stepped forward, waiting for instructions.

"We'll see," Cricket said softly, and then focused her attention on Medusa.

Cricket was a native Hawaiian, and today, as usual, her long black hair was caught up in a messy bun skewered in place by an ivory chopstick. At least, it *had* been.

Though she was almost always cool under pressure, Cricket's bun had started to slip, and her thick glasses were askew.

"What a ride. My guess was wrong," she said, studying the mare. "I kept weighing the differences between an open trailer and a closed one, and finally Luke—our vet—flipped a coin and we went with the open trailer."

"She woulda hated it either way." Kit sounded hypnotized, and he still hadn't greeted his girlfriend. He watched Medusa.

The mare's coat was nearly black with sweat. Clots of foam coated her mouth and muzzle.

"Let's get her outta there," Kit said.

The mare wore a lightweight halter, and ropes came away from it on each side.

"If we hadn't cross-tied her, she would've climbed out," Cricket said.

Kit gestured for Cade to take the far rope while he untied the near one.

Without Kit's instructions, Cricket moved to the critical position behind the mare to open the trailer door. Darby and Megan stood by, but they backed up to give the others room.

Since the mare's kicks were already resounding against the metal, Cricket didn't get too close until Cade and Kit had dodged Medusa's teeth and grabbed the ropes on either side of her halter.

"Poor girl," Darby murmured.

"I don't even want to see her legs." Megan winced, then noticed Jonah walking in their direction from the tack shed. "Here comes Jonah with the first-aid kit, but I don't know how they're going to get close enough to use it."

Medusa's neck curved toward Cade. She stood for a moment, then lunged with bared teeth for his hand. As he jumped back, Cade inadvertently gave the mare a little more rope. Instantly she took up the slack by bending like a dog after its tail.

"She's trying to turn," Cade said. He shortened the

length of rope once more, but Medusa was determined to leave the trailer headfirst instead of backing out.

"She just doesn't get it," Darby said.

"Can she make it if I slack off on this side? It looks like she can." Kit kept his voice level.

Cade bobbed into range of the mare, checking to see whether there was space enough for her to escape the trailer frontward.

The mare's open mouth went for his head.

Cade's hala hat spun off as he ducked and said, "Think so."

Cricket nodded at Kit, who gave Medusa the rope she needed to turn around. Holding the trailer door open, Cricket dodged behind it, shielding herself from Medusa.

"I'm okay," Cricket reassured Kit.

With the way clear before her, the mare charged out toward Sun House.

Her legs *were* bleeding. Darby heard Cricket's frustrated grunt. Even as Medusa hit the end of the twin ropes restraining her, Cricket was walking around the mare, trying to study her legs.

Megan gasped at Cricket's bravery, then said, "She totally trusts those guys to hold on."

Shining with sweat, the gray mare gave short dolphin leaps forward, dragging Cade and Kit.

"She's reopened some stitches." Cricket sounded both sad and disgusted.

During the tsunami, Darby had watched on

horseback with Kit and Cade as Black Lava and Medusa swam their herd out to a lava spit for safety. But once the storm was over, the horses had been coaxed back to land. Only Medusa had refused to follow.

Kit had used his bronc-riding skills to climb onto the mare's back and stuff cotton into her ears to dull the roar of helicopters overhead. Only when the mare had swum ashore and stood shivering beneath a sodden black mane had they noticed her legs, bleeding from cuts on the lava rock.

"She's all yours," Cricket joked feebly.

"Ideas?" Kit grunted as the mare made another hop, pulling his boot heels through the dirt.

"Let her up."

Darby sucked in a breath, pretty sure Cricket wanted to calm the mare with fewer restrictions. But they couldn't let her get away. Running with trailing ropes and bleeding legs would be disastrous.

As Medusa reared, pawing the air with outrage, Kit and Cade let out the ropes. Confused by her head's freedom, the mare touched her front hooves down, tossed her mane and forelock from her face, then reared again.

Foam flew from her lips, and for a single instant her eyes rolled until they showed a bit of red rim.

Darby stepped back so quickly her boot crunched down on Jonah's.

"Remember that," he said quietly. He pointed, but

the mare's eyes had already returned to normal.

"Can we tranquilize her?" Cade asked.

Darby looked at Kit, then Cricket and Jonah. None of them answered him, but Darby guessed they didn't want to traumatize the mare any further.

"I have some of Tutu's concoction left," Cade said. "The stuff she made up for Honi."

"Sounds good," Kit said, but his voice was so quiet Darby didn't know whether Cade heard.

"Is it still in your poncho?" Megan asked, and when Cade nodded, she darted for the bunkhouse.

Medusa couldn't maintain her rearing balance much longer. The mare's back legs trembled. One hoof stepped forward. Finally she stood on all fours again, front legs spread wide. Her head hung low, and her forelock veiled her face, down to her nostrils.

Just as Megan returned, Aunty Cathy came out of the office. Face flushed with exertion, she carried a bucket that sloshed water over its sides.

"I couldn't stay away," Aunty Cathy said. "Look at her. She's exhausted."

Medusa stumbled backward a step, and though her head still hung low, she moved it up slowly, watching all the humans staring at her.

Looking sweaty and spent, Cade sighted across the horse's back. He raised his eyebrows at Megan. She held up a packet wrapped in waxed paper. It must be the herbs Tutu had left for Honi.

Cade nodded, and Megan sprinkled the herbs over

the surface of the water in the bucket.

"I thought you were supposed to let her eat it, or rub it on her gums or something," Darby whispered to Megan.

Megan looked up. Her mocking smile wrinkled her nose a little as she said, "You go first."

Darby laughed at herself. "Yeah, I guess that's not going to happen."

Even though the mare was exhausted, Darby doubted anyone could get close enough to touch her mouth, and the steeldust wasn't trusting enough to take food from their hands.

As Megan finished stirring the herbs around with her fingers, Cricket crouched beside her.

"We'll let it steep a few minutes, like tea. Then, since she's most familiar with me, I'll bring her the bucket. She must be thirsty, and even if it doesn't sedate her much—" Cricket broke off and turned to Darby and asked, "Body weight?"

"Uhh . . ."

"Compare Honi the pony and Medusa," Cricket explained. "I haven't seen Honi for a while, and we need to be cautious. Medusa was hard bodied and lean when she came into the rescue barn, and she's even thinner now. Dosage, even with herbal remedies, is based on body weight. So, what do you think?"

"I'd say they're close to the same," Darby ventured. "Honi's fit, but a little, you know, round."

Cricket nodded and stared into the bucket carefully.

She might have been reading tea leaves.

Jonah, Aunty Cathy, and Megan were standing right there. Why hadn't she asked one of them? Darby wondered. Still, she felt proud knowing Cricket trusted her skills of observation.

Darby's gaze was on Kit as Cricket approached with the bucket. Kit's hands didn't tighten on the rope. He didn't dig in his boots for more traction, and he didn't caution the young woman as she set the bucket near enough to Medusa that she could drink. Or bite. Or kick.

Kit's face was the only part of him that showed his tension, and his relief as Cricket backed away.

Medusa tried to ignore the bucket. She took a few steps past it until the ropes were taut once more. She stood at the apex of a triangle, with the ropes leading back to Cade on one side and Kit on the other.

But she was thirsty. Her mouth opened and closed. Her lips moved. Her head lifted and her nostrils quivered as she smelled the water.

"She knows buckets now. She's not afraid. And there's no reason to stay silent. She's being stubborn." Cricket whispered, but Medusa pinned her ears at the human voice.

I don't know how Kit's going to gentle her, Darby thought. *From the first, Hoku liked the sound of my storytelling.* And then she remembered something Jonah had said.

"What did you mean before when you said, 'Remember that'?" Darby asked her grandfather.

"Did you catch the way she rolled her eyes so you could almost see the rims?" he asked.

"Uh-huh."

"I've *never* seen a mare act that way. Not even your tomboy."

Kit nodded in agreement as Jonah went on. "Warring stallions will do that. It's threatenin' body language. The strongest. When a stallion rolls his eyes like that, he's promising a fight to the death."

"She sees us as attackers, not rescuers." Kit said it matter-of-factly to the others, but the corners of his mouth drooped, as if he'd just realized how long it would take to show the mare that he was on her side.

Medusa fought her thirst as long as she could, then lowered her head to the bucket and drank deeply. An hour later, she allowed herself to be half-dragged, half-chased down to Hoku's corral.

"Leave the ropes on," Jonah said. "She's still gotta be doctored, and I don't see those plants knocking her out."

They had closed the mare in, with all the humans outside, when Kimo rode Biscuit in from the fold at the end of the road.

Medusa snorted, tossed her forelock away from her eyes, and stumbled closer to the fence.

Sizing up the situation, Kimo ordered the dogs to stay, then rode a bit closer and ground-tied the buckskin horse near the corral.

Biscuit's ears twitched in all directions, and he returned Medusa's snort. He dragged his reins a few feet and extended his nose toward the fence before glancing at Aunty Cathy.

"You're fine, boy," Aunty Cathy said, and Darby remembered the horse had belonged to her husband, Ben. "Just keep Medusa company."

Biscuit lipped a weed that had grown up near the corral since Hoku's absence, and Medusa snapped at him. Even though she was clumsy from the effect of the herbs, she let him know she was still a lead mare.

"Not a real promisin' start," Kit said warily. "I'm inclined to set her free."

Darby was surprised, but it took her only a second to realize that Black Lava and his band couldn't have gone far. Medusa could rejoin her herd!

"This is something you can't do halfway," Cricket said. She sounded highly professional, as if she were addressing any other wild horse adopter. "We brought her in injured, stitched her up, and now she's opened the wounds and has to heal all over again. In the wild . . ."

Cricket stopped. Maybe she was tired, but Darby thought Cricket didn't want to harass Kit by pointing out that Medusa's injuries would, at best, handicap her.

At worst, she could bleed to death or get an infection.

"She's not going to be the lead mare again like she

was," Darby said, and the idea brought a lump to her throat.

"That'd be hard for her," Kit said.

Aunty Cathy turned from exchanging a look with Jonah and said, "Let's keep her here for a couple weeks."

A couple weeks! Darby thought, in despair, of Hoku. But she saw Jonah's slight nod.

Jonah had no use for any animal that didn't earn its keep. He didn't have lots of loose cash around to pay for Medusa's feed, either. But he valued Kit and trusted him to make the right decision, so he was letting the steeldust stay. He was even ready to risk injury to himself to treat hers.

"After that," Aunty Cathy went on, "she should be pretty much healed. And she should be starting to adjust. If you don't feel like she's fitting in by then . . ."

Aunty Cathy left the sentence dangling, but Kimo finished it.

"Aloha."

That night before bed, Darby phoned Ann.

"We have to come up with *something* for English," Darby said, getting right to the point when Ann answered.

"I know!" Ann replied. "Let me get the sheet Ms. Day gave us at the beginning of the year. It lists what we can do for our second-semester final presentation." Ann rustled some papers and came back on the line.

"Well, we're down to two bad choices, but at least we can do these together."

"I'm bracing myself," Darby said.

"We can do a Food Channel–style cooking demonstration . . ."

"Can't cook at all," Darby remarked.

" . . . or compose an original song and perform it in front of the class."

"That's all?" Darby asked. "We're in big trouble."

"No, we're not." Ann sounded as if she were chiding a child.

"You can get a new partner if it's not too late," Darby offered, "because the only thing I'm worse at than cooking is singing."

"Everybody can sing," Ann insisted.

"That's what you think," Darby said.

There was silence on the line for a moment before Ann asked, "Which rodeo events does Jonah want us to enter?"

"No!" Darby cried. "Don't distract me! We can't talk about the rodeo until we pick a project! If I'm ever going to get my mother to move to Hawaii I *need* an A."

"I knew that would work," Ann said, laughing. "Now, I'm up for singing or cooking. I don't care which. You pick."

"I guess cooking is less horrible," Darby said.

"Okay!"

"You don't have to sound so"—Darby fumbled for a

word—"*peppy* about it."

"I am peppy! I've got all A's going into finals, and I'm excited about the rodeo! Life is sweet!"

"Well, I'm really tired, and I've still got to study some more for Ecology."

"I'll quiz you," Ann said, since she was in the same class.

Twenty minutes later, as she was saying good-bye to Ann, Darby felt pretty confident.

Finals were just big tests. She could do this.

She assembled all of the books, pens, pencils, and paper she'd need for her first day of finals and put them on the bench by the front door.

Before trying to sleep, she got out her diary and wrote about Medusa.

She has the heart of a lion, and I wonder if it's too late to ever tame her. I know Kit loves her, but I'm pretty certain he'd let her go if he thought it was best for her. Could I do that for Hoku? I don't think so. Forget that—I know I couldn't. Does that mean I love Hoku less than Kit loves Medusa? That can't possibly be true.
Except, oh, my gosh.

Darby dropped her pencil. It slipped off the bed and rolled across her bedroom floor.

She hadn't gone down to the pasture to see Hoku today! With studying, Medusa, and everything else, she'd put it off until it was too late to go.

Her heart thudded against the inside of her chest like something trying to get out.

How could she have left Hoku down there, listening to the cries of a wild horse? What if Black Lava had kidnapped her yesterday and she wasn't even on the ranch anymore?

She would have guessed her thoughts couldn't have gotten any darker, but then they did.

Kanaka Luna's threatening neigh was carried on the breeze through her open bedroom window. Thread thin and faraway, it still sounded ferocious, and it gave Darby chills, especially since it was followed by a troubled whinny from one of the mares.

Why weren't the dogs barking? If a strange person or a predator had come onto the ranch they'd be raising a commotion. But they had been well trained to leave the horses alone.

Did that mean that the threat Kanaka Luna was warning against was another horse? A memory leaped into Darby's mind. It was of the night, not long after she'd first arrived, when she saw the fabled Shining Stallion out her window, under the candlenut tree.

She perched on her knees to look out the window. Starlight painted the candlenut tree's leaves silver, but that was all.

Swinging her legs to the floor, she stuck her diary into its drawer and pulled on a sweatshirt. She'd nearly made it to the front door when Jonah opened it.

From the outside.

"What's up?" she asked him.

"That stud's got rocks in his head, is all," Jonah told her. "Carrying on about nothing. I walked all the way down to his pasture and back."

Something had to be wrong, Darby thought. Her guilt about Hoku hadn't made that neigh sound distressed. And Jonah's night vision wasn't the best.

Darby didn't know what to say. She hadn't been able to shake off her uneasiness with Jonah since yesterday. She'd been careful, because she didn't want to make him mad, and sympathetic because of his failing eyesight. It wasn't a good combination.

Jonah was watching her shift from one bare foot to the other.

"Put on some slippers"—he spotted a pair of Megan's, under the bench, and nudged them toward Darby—"and go check things out."

One thing Darby loved about life on the ranch was the way Jonah treated her like any other working member. He relied on her to make sensible decisions, and trusted her almost like another adult.

Darby was sliding her feet into the slippers—she would have called them flip-flops if she still lived in California—when Jonah planted a quick kiss on her hair.

She looked up in surprise and Jonah scowled at her.

"Come get me if you need me. I never get eight

hours of sleep, anyway," he grumbled. "Why should tonight be any different?"

Darby paused on the front steps and listened to the night.

Other than an ocean breeze that rustled the leaves of the candlenut tree, everything was silent. In fact, it seemed unusually still, as if she'd stepped into a room where people had been talking about her, and they'd stopped when she entered.

She thought of the crazy owl that had scared her yesterday, and curled one arm over her head as she walked toward the tack room.

Just then a light inside the foreman's house blinked on. Kit or Cade must have heard Luna, too.

Inside the corral, Medusa was illuminated by the light from the front window. The mare stood at the corral fence. The bandages on her legs showed, and her ears pricked forward to catch the slightest sound.

Darby headed toward the corral. No moonlight lit her way and the brightness falling from the foreman's house window didn't reach this far. Rushing through the darkness, she stepped right out of Megan's too-big slippers, then crashed the bare arch of her foot on a rock in her path. She staggered but managed not to yelp.

Both slippers on, or both off? Darby decided flimsy protection was better than none. Then, as soon as she'd jammed her feet into the slippers, she remembered a night-vision trick Cade had taught her. Standing still, she closed her eyes and covered them with both hands.

Out in the rain forest, waiting for the appearance of a rabid boar, he'd told her, *The longer it is since I've looked into the light, the better I can see in the dark.*

When she took her hands away, she saw something move. Beyond the fox cages and past the corral, at the end of the road, a shadow wavered.

She hardly dared to breathe.

It had to be Black Lava. He'd discovered Medusa was at the ranch and had come back for her. He didn't know she couldn't jump the fence or run beside him. He didn't know that tempting her to follow was cruel.

With silent steps, Black Lava approached the corral.

There was no mistaking the touching of noses over the fence and the low nickers. They had missed each other. They were delighted in this reunion.

Medusa pushed against the fence, and the stallion pushed back. Medusa shoved her chest against the fence again, and Black Lava did, too. It was a strong fence, reinforced for Hoku, but could two horses working together break it down?

Kit burst from the foreman's house and the dogs began barking.

Black Lava shied, and Darby heard the dirt and gravel slip under his churning hooves. He disappeared, though Medusa ran around the corral, trying to build up speed. The white bandages on her front legs went up and down as she charged at the fence.

Darby drew in a sharp breath, sure Medusa would jump.

Could her injured legs carry her? Darby didn't think so.

At the last second Medusa veered away from the fence, not daring to go over.

Black Lava whinnied. From where? Darby couldn't see the stallion calling for Medusa to try again.

Kit grabbed the pitchfork leaning against one wall of the tack shed and stormed forward.

"You get!" he shouted, waving the pitchfork.

The dogs barked even louder, and Darby heard them hit the side of their kennel as they followed the stallion's movement. Closer now, Darby saw that Black Lava had retreated to the other side of the corral, but he wasn't going anywhere.

Medusa battered her chest against the corral gate, sensing where it should give.

Black Lava circled the corral at a run. Even when he faced Kit and the pitchfork, the stallion didn't falter. In an onslaught of hooves and horsehide, he forced the foreman to let him pass.

Kit could have jabbed the horse, but he didn't, and Darby guessed Kit had sized up the situation just as she had. Black Lava understood Medusa must be left behind. Without hesitating, the black mustang raced alone into the darkness.

Medusa called after him, frantic for her mate to return. Her neigh rose and fell, again and again.

After such chaos, the stallion wouldn't come back, Darby thought. Didn't Medusa know that?

Kit replaced the pitchfork, then faced Medusa. The mare crossed the corral, stopped to listen, then made her way to the other side and listened again.

Kit held out a hand, but he was invisible to her. Medusa's hopeless prowling went on after Kit turned back to the bunkhouse, after Cade returned from the broodmare pasture to say all the horses, including Hoku, were safe. Long after Darby had gone inside Sun House, the sounds of searching carried on the breeze through her window.

 Chapter Six

The next morning, Darby stared blankly into her school locker and yawned. After she'd gone back inside and talked about Medusa with Jonah, she'd tried to sleep.

But she couldn't.

Medusa had trotted back and forth in the corral all night, neighing for Black Lava to come back. Even after Darby got up and shut the window, she could still hear the wild mare's distressed cries. When fitful sleep finally came, she dreamed that Hoku was in trouble.

In the dream, Darby wandered the ranch, searching for Hoku in empty pastures, in vine-choked Crimson Vale, and on barren, windswept beaches. She could hear Hoku in the dream, but she never found her.

She awoke frustrated and exhausted. Only when she'd leaned out on the lanai, staring over the pastures for a glimpse of Hoku, and saw her, did Darby start getting ready for school.

Megan had groaned at Darby's slowness, saying she'd strangle her if Darby made them late for their first final, but they'd not only made it on time, they were fifteen minutes early.

"Were you up all night?" asked Ann. Her wild red curls bounced as she blocked an avalanche of books plummeting from Darby's locker.

"*Almost* all night. When I finally fell asleep I had the worst dreams."

As they walked to Ecology, Darby told Ann about the wild horses' reunion.

"It's kind of romantic," Ann said, tilting her head toward Darby. "How did Black Lava even know she was there?"

Darby shook her head. "Smell? Sixth sense? I don't know."

"That's why I love horses so much," Ann said. "Just when you start thinking it's all about picking up poop and digging dirt out of their feet, they do something magical and spooky. Like this."

Darby would have agreed, except that they'd reached the doorway to Ecology and a boy named Tyson was blocking their way.

Darby stiffened. For some reason Tyson loved to tease her. No, she corrected herself, it had gone beyond teasing. One day he'd make fun of her because she'd embraced her new culture with excitement. The next day he'd act like she had no right to island customs, since she wasn't one hundred percent Hawaiian.

Whatever the reason, he was a real pain. Ann shoved past him, careful not to touch him with her armload of books, but he made a huge uproar by pretending to fall over a trash can.

Darby asked, "Why are you so awful all the time?"

"Because he has the brains of a mongoose," Ann suggested.

"That's being generous," Darby snapped.

Tyson gave a self-satisfied laugh and headed for his desk in the back of the room.

When Darby and Ann sat down, Ann began brushing at the front of her blouse.

"Sugar," she mumbled. "All over the . . ."

At her friend's sudden silence, Darby looked up from her book.

"I know what we're going to cook," Ann said. She picked a single crystal of sugar from her shirt and held it so close to Darby's face that her eyes crossed.

"What?" Darby asked, sitting back before Ann made her dizzy.

"Malasadas!" Ann crowed. "That's what this is from," she said, brushing the front of her shirt again. "Mom stopped at a malasada truck on the way in, but hers are even better."

"We could demonstrate how to *make* malasadas?" Darby asked, but she was already picturing the sugar-coated, deep-fried pastry.

"Aunty Cathy makes them so well you can hardly believe it. Come over after school and we'll get her recipe. . . ."

Before they could celebrate their anticipated A's in English, their Ecology teacher entered wearing a flapping white lab coat. As he passed out the tests, they forgot everything else.

Ann finished the final exam early and started writing their Food Network–style script.

"I can finish this next period," Ann promised Darby as they filed out of Ecology. "Since I'm an office aide, I won't be taking a test. But how are we going to make them in class without a stove?"

"Aunty Cathy makes them in an electric frying pan," Darby said. "At least, I think so. I'm always too busy eating to really pay attention to how she does it."

"We'll work it out. I'll call my mom and tell her I'm going home with you to study," Ann said. "Okay? And while we work on the malasadas, we can talk about the rodeo!"

"Definitely," Darby agreed, and then she ran down the hall toward the gym, hoping her P.E. test really was the "piece of cake" Megan had promised.

❋ ❋ ❋

It turned out that Ann had to go home and help put Sugarfoot in his corral before she could come over to 'Iolani Ranch.

The caramel-and-white pinto was a problem horse, Ann admitted, but since she and her mother had been working with him he was improving, and Ann's mother promised she'd bring Ann over to practice making malasadas as soon as she could.

Darby wasn't entirely sad about the change in plans.

On the drive to 'Iolani Ranch, Aunty Cathy had agreed to help with the malasada project. She'd make sure they had all the ingredients, set up the electric frying pan, and simplify the recipe—even though, she'd said pointedly, it was a pretty last-minute arrangement.

As soon as she got home, Darby changed into her old jeans and her red sweatshirt with the cutoff sleeves. She was going down to visit Hoku no matter what.

She was nearly out the front door when the kitchen phone rang.

She made a growling noise, since she knew she was alone.

Jonah was down by Hoku's corral with Kit checking on Medusa. Aunty Cathy and Megan had just gone upstairs, so Darby gave in and grabbed the phone.

"Darby, I'm glad I caught you," Cricket said. "Would you and Megan be willing to join a group of volunteers who are riding rain-forest and grasslands paths, trying to keep Black Lava and his herd from returning to Crimson Vale? They've been seen in the area and seem to be trying to get back."

Impatient to reach Hoku, Darby didn't tell Cricket how much she'd seen of Black Lava the last few days. She simply asked, "Why not just let them return?"

"The water hasn't been certified potable yet," Cricket replied.

Potable equaled *drinkable*, Darby was pretty sure, but Cricket took the gap in conversation as confusion.

"That's why we drove them up Sky Mountain in the first place, remember? Of course you do," Cricket answered herself.

Maybe if Darby hadn't seen Black Lava's wild desperation with her own eyes, she would have agreed to help. But she had.

Still, she respected Cricket too much to argue with her, so she made an excuse.

"I'll have to ask Jonah," Darby said. "I'll tell Megan about it, too."

"Okay," Cricket said, but she knew she was being put off. "Kit told me what happened last night with Black Lava."

"Oh."

"Seems to me we'd be doing a good deed for the horses and your grandfather."

"I'll talk to him," Darby promised. Then, feeling a

little weird, she said good-bye to Cricket, hung up the phone, and sat on the bench to put on her boots.

Because she didn't want to make Hoku jealous, Darby walked toward the broodmare pasture instead of riding. She hadn't gone far when Jonah came out from the tack room.

"You ever going to change the shavings in that Pigolo's pen?" Jonah asked.

Darby nodded. She couldn't utter a word of complaint, since she'd been the one to lecture the family about pigs being as clean as people allowed them to be.

"And Francie?" Jonah said, gesturing toward the black-and-white goat dozing by Sun House. "That goat doesn't like her new hay. Better ask Cathy what Cricket said to do about it."

Darby agreed to do everything, especially since Jonah hadn't mentioned his plans for barbecuing one of the animals on Fourth of July, and then she told him about her conversation with Cricket.

He shrugged. "I think Kit scared him good."

"I hope so," Darby said. "Do you think he went back to Sky Mountain?"

"He'd be a fool to do that if Snowfire's taken his pick of his mares."

Darby was just about to head down the hill to her horse when Jonah put his rough hand on her shoulder. "Cathy's going back into town. Said she had to pick up a big jug of cooking oil—"

That would be for the malasadas, Darby thought guiltily.

"—and stop in at the feed store. Cricket talked to her about some special hay cubes for your goat, but she forgot them when she was picking you girls up. I guess the test schedule threw her off."

Darby didn't ask how Francie had turned into *her* goat. She just said, "I was going down to work with Hoku."

"I'll help you with that later," Kit shouted across the ranch yard.

Great, Darby thought.

Jonah crossed his arms. "Cathy needs your help."

Darby knew better than to object. Cathy was helping her, so she had to help Cathy. "Okay," Darby said, heading toward the ranch truck.

"There she is," Aunty Cathy said to Megan, who was apparently coming, too. "Just in time to go *back* into town."

As they drove, Darby recounted Cricket's request that they join other volunteers in blocking Black Lava and his herd's return to Crimson Vale.

"I hope Jonah's right that he's taken his herd back up to Sky Mountain," she said. "I hate to say no to Cricket, but it just doesn't feel right to keep blocking Black Lava like that."

"It's for the good of the horses," Aunty Cathy reminded her.

"But they don't like Sky Mountain," Darby said. "I think Snowfire . . . Well, I'm not sure what's happening up there, but I know Black Lava had three foals before, and now he only has one."

When Aunty Cathy looked up in the rearview mirror to meet Darby's eyes, she was frowning.

Aunty Cathy parked outside the feed store, and they hurried inside.

The store smelled like some kind of exotic breakfast food. They wended their way through aisles stacked to the ceiling with burlap bags, but when they reached Cricket's office, in the back, they learned she'd left early.

According to a clerk, Cricket had to make arrangements for an animal rescue, but she had left a sample bag of goat chow for Francie.

Darby didn't say a word about Cricket's absence, but she was a little relieved. She didn't want to defend her reluctance to frighten Black Lava off the trails to Crimson Vale.

Aunty Cathy ran across the street to the grocery store for malasada supplies, while Darby and Megan loaded the dog food and Francie's new goat chow on a handcart and wheeled it out to the truck.

Darby and Megan pitched the heavy sacks into the back of the vehicle.

"Thank you, ladies," Aunty Cathy said as they all climbed back inside.

Traffic was heavier than usual when they reached the road. "The tourist season is starting," Aunty Cathy noted. "And there'll be even more people in time for the rodeo."

"That doesn't sound good," Darby replied.

"I've been thinking about Black Lava's foals," Aunty Cathy said. This time when she met Darby's eyes in the mirror, she looked sympathetic. "In fact, I bumped into Cricket at the market, picking up a sandwich for her dinner, and told her about the herd."

They were nearly out of the small downtown area, and Aunty Cathy picked up speed as she turned onto the main road leading toward the ranch.

"And what did she say?" Megan asked.

"Does she think the trip to Sky Mountain was just too much for them?" Darby suggested.

"Nothing like that," Aunty Cathy said carefully. "Apparently wild stallions . . . Well, sometimes when they steal each other's mares, they kill their foals."

"No way!" Megan said. "Why?"

But Darby had already figured it out, or maybe Samantha, back in Nevada, had once hinted at the awful behavior. "Survival of the fittest?" Darby asked.

Aunty Cathy nodded. "The strongest stallion wants *his* babies to live, so when he steals a mare, he does away with her foal. Sometimes he even injures mares who are expecting foals, so that the old stallion's young won't be born."

"That's awful," Megan said.

"Here we go." Aunty Cathy accelerated, maybe as a distraction, or because she was relieved that the pace of the cars around them had picked up.

One of the feed sacks in the back slid off the pile and crashed down to the side.

Startled, Aunty Cathy swiveled a half turn in her seat to see what had happened. "What was—"

"Mom! Look out!" Megan shouted.

 Chapter Seven

Darby barely believed what she saw through the front windshield.

Black Lava's herd was running across the road!

Aunty Cathy jammed to an abrupt stop. Darby lurched forward. The feed sacks slammed behind her, and for a moment she was afraid she'd be folded in half by the seat back. Her seat belt jerked tight across her shoulder and chest.

The vehicle fishtailed. Brakes squealed. A horn blared from somewhere outside. And then they stopped.

The truck was filled with feed dust. Darby batted at the powder swirling in front of her eyes.

The horses were still right in front of them. A

screech made Darby turn and stare through the back window. A silver car—

"Don't hit us!" Darby shouted. Could a collision push them into the horses?

When the car behind them stopped clear of them, Darby unsnapped her seat belt and leaned forward to get a better look at the horses.

Terrified by the squealing, smoking tires and machines, the small black foal had crashed into the back of the mare in front of him. She wasn't his mother, and she was angry. She turned and clacked her teeth at him so loudly, Darby could hear the sound inside the car.

Seeing her colt in trouble, his bay mother ran between the chestnut mare and the colt. The chestnut bumped the bay, sending her into a panicked slide before she fell to her knees.

"Everybody okay?" Aunty Cathy's question sounded more like a demand. Once Megan and Darby both said yes, Aunty Cathy was out of the vehicle, heading toward the horses.

"Mom! What do you think you're doing!" Megan shouted.

Black Lava snorted. The bay's hooves scrambled on asphalt as she pulled herself upright, then led her foal off the street and into the forest, following the other mares.

For a few crazy heartbeats, Darby watched Black Lava stand guard at the pavement's edge, giving his herd time to escape. And then he must have stepped back-ward into the foliage, because suddenly he was gone.

When Darby and Megan joined Aunty Cathy out-side the truck, a vehicle two cars back from theirs had begun honking its horn, not realizing what was caus-ing the delay.

Aunty Cathy quickly made sure that the driver who had nearly collided with her—an elderly man in khaki shorts and a colorful Hawaiian shirt—was not injured, and then rushed back to the girls.

Darby and Megan were shaking feed dust out of their hair and rubbing their watery eyes. Aunty Cathy asked again if they were hurt.

"No. We've just got all this dust in our eyes," Darby said.

"Okay, then let's go. We're blocking traffic."

"Why was that idiot horse bringing his herd across the road?" Megan yelled.

"Megan—" Aunty Cathy began.

"Every safe path he wants to take is blocked!" Darby snapped.

"Girls—"

"That's the idea!" Megan shouted at Darby. "So he can't go drink poison water!"

"Yeah, look what it's doing! If your mom hadn't stopped in time, they'd be dead anyway!"

Aunty Cathy placed her thumb and a finger in the corners of her mouth, and gave a shrill whistle.

Darby and Megan stared at her.

"That's better," she said gently. "We're all safe. The horses weren't hurt, and neither was the truck. You're not mad at each other. Not really. You're just a little bit scared."

"I'm not . . ." Both girls started to deny the statement, then stopped.

Darby thought of Medusa, covering up fear with fury. Darby met Megan's brown eyes. They both shrugged.

Aunty Cathy hustled them back into the truck, restarted it, and drove straight down the proper lane, even though her hands were shaking on the wheel.

Even though she rode in silence with Megan and Aunty Cathy, Darby's mind was anything but quiet.

Black Lava would not stay on Sky Mountain. She was sure of it now. No wild stallion walked across a busy highway if he had another choice.

Snowfire couldn't be blamed for driving a younger stallion off his territory, but the white stallion was the problem. She'd seen him chasing Black Lava and his herd off the ridge. The chase had lasted for only a moment, but she'd known what it meant.

Back when she'd lived in Pacific Pinnacles Darby hadn't known about listening to what her heart told her. But coming to Hawaii had changed things.

Both Jonah and Tutu had told her to trust her mana—that which she'd learned from books, people, and experience—and her *māna*—the truth she was born knowing.

Both were telling her that Black Lava and his herd should be allowed to go home.

Several times in the past Cricket had asked Darby her opinions about horses.

Darby really hoped Cricket would trust her this time.

When they arrived back at Sun House, Darby immediately phoned the rescue barn and asked for Cricket.

While she waited, Darby realized that dinner was being prepared around her.

"I'll take my turn," she promised quietly. "And oh! We're going to be practicing making malasadas, so we'll need some volunteer tasters."

Aunty Cathy and Megan laughed way too much at her offer, and Darby was wondering if it was some kind of reaction to the near accident when she thought of Ann.

Oh, my gosh! Ann was supposed to have come over after she'd gotten Sugarfoot back in his pen. Had Ann and her mother driven all the way over to 'Iolani Ranch, only to find it deserted?

But then Cricket was on the phone, and Darby told her, carefully and calmly and in front of two witnesses—neither of whom contradicted her—what had happened.

Over the phone, Darby heard the clash of metal buckets and a door closing at the rescue barn.

"That's why I hesitated when you asked me to join

the volunteers on the paths," Darby admitted when Cricket said nothing. "If he's, uh, crossing streets and, well, trying to go between cars to get home . . . I don't know. Do you . . ." Darby swallowed hard. She wasn't a know-it-all, and she didn't want to sound like one, but she had to ask. "Do you really think we'll keep those horses out of Crimson Vale?"

Cricket released a long sigh. There was a rustling sound against the telephone receiver, and Darby pictured Cricket rewinding her bun and stabbing it through with something to hold it in place.

"Some riders are already pushing the herd back toward Sky Mountain."

"Oh, no," Darby said.

"I'll call the conservancy and see if I can get in touch with the wildlife biologist," she said at last. "I'll tell him what happened and ask if he can do an emergency water test."

"Thank you," Darby said.

"Don't expect an overnight miracle," Cricket cautioned. "Between the earthquakes and the tsunami, this guy is busy. He doesn't always return my calls right away."

What if it's too late? Darby thought.

Black Lava had only a few mares and one foal left. Snowfire wasn't the only danger to them. Wasting time could mean wasting the wild horses' lives.

But none of this was Cricket's fault, so Darby stayed quiet.

"I'll do my best, Darby," Cricket promised. "And just to prepare you—if they test the water and it's still bad . . ."

"I know."

"I'm glad no one—two- or four-footed—was hurt. I'll call the conservancy as soon as I hang up, and get back to you the minute I hear anything. I have the phone numbers for two landlines and three cell phones on that ranch," Cricket joked.

"Thank you," Darby replied. "Bye."

She sat like a zombie through dinner. Why wouldn't her brain give her a solution?

She needed evidence to sway the conservancy's biologist.

The best way to get that would be to observe the stallion and his herd in the new home that they were so stubbornly refusing to settle into.

Dessert was almost on the table when Jonah waved a hand in front of Darby's face.

"Cathy told me what happened. You're okay, yeah?"

She nodded. "I'm fine."

"Good."

"Could I go camping on Sky Mountain?" she blurted, surprising herself as well as Jonah. "That way I could see what the problem is, figure out why Black Lava doesn't want to keep his herd up there."

"No—"

"I wouldn't go alone. I'd get . . . Ann. Yes, Ann

would go with me, I bet."

"Darby Leilani, think. If you got into trouble, what would Ann do? You've got two warring stallions up there, and even if you resisted trying to help them—which you would not!—" He broke off, shaking his head, and added, "Wasn't seeing Medusa enough to show you the wild horses you love can be dangerous?"

"I know!" Darby yelped. "You could go with us! You could take us camping up there and show us all the cool stuff! I bet you haven't been up there in years; am I right? It would be fun!"

Jonah scowled. He was on the verge of refusing, she was sure of it, but then his face softened. "It *might* be fun," he conceded. "I haven't been camping in a while."

"You'll really do it?" Darby jumped out of her chair so quickly it fell over backward, and both Aunty Cathy and Megan looked in from the kitchen to see what was happening. "Jonah's going to take me camping on Sky Mountain!"

She hugged Megan around the neck.

"Don't practice your bulldogging on me," Megan protested, but she was smiling as she pushed Darby away.

"I can't guarantee you we'll see any horses," Jonah cautioned. "And I'm not going on a wild-goose chase searching for them, either."

"No goose chases—or even wild-horse chases.

Promise." Darby had never made such a devout cross over her heart.

"We can only go for one night," he added. "I can't abandon this place, yeah?"

"One night would be awesome," she assured him, not wanting anything to make him change his mind.

"So, you're clear. We might not even see wild horses?"

"Completely clear. Crystal clear!" Darby barely kept herself from dancing.

"And that's okay?"

"If we don't see horses, we don't see them. At least we'll have tried, and we'll have some fun, anyway. I've never been camping with my grandpa."

He pointed his index finger at her in a way that seemed to say, *Don't start*, so Darby put both hands over her mouth.

"Okay then," he agreed. "You can look at the trip as a little end-of-the-school-year reward, a break before those tourists descend on us to ride all Babe's pretty horses."

"I know we'll have a wonderful time," Darby said, wrapping her grandfather in a quick hug. Despite all his warnings and disclaimers, she had confidence in Jonah's skills in tracking wild horses. She knew they'd discover why Black Lava was so set on returning to Crimson Vale. "Can I call Ann and tell her? And Mom, too?"

❈ ❈ ❈

Thursday was another shortened school day because of finals, and, despite the two-hour tests—Creative Writing and Algebra—Darby felt great.

She was determined to spend part of her day with Hoku. Kit had carved some time out of his schedule to help her before Ann—who hadn't made it over to 'Iolani Ranch yesterday because they hadn't trapped Sugarfoot until after dark—came over to practice tomorrow's presentation.

Never before had Darby thrown off her school outfit and jumped into riding clothes so fast. She swept her hair up into a fresh ponytail, ready to signal Hoku that they were partners again.

She located Kit in the tack room, putting the lid on an unlabeled jar.

"Tutu's favorite herb poultice goo," he said, holding it up. "I rode over to talk to her, and she mixed it up for Medusa's cuts."

"How's she doing?" Darby asked.

Kit shook his head. "Still loco to get outta here."

"Do you want to release her?" Darby asked.

"Do I *want* to, or am I *gonna*?" he asked her back. "Right now she wouldn't make it. She'd die trying." Kit cleared his throat. "Just have to wait 'n' see."

He pulled Hoku's halter and orange-striped lead rope down from a hook and handed them to her. "You go catch your horse. I'll be down after my own private rodeo."

Darby didn't stay to watch him doctor Medusa. She hurried down the dirt road to the pasture. Her left shoulder hurt from the quick grab of the seat belt yesterday, but the pain was nothing compared to the way her heart sang at the sight of her sorrel mustang grazing out in the field, not far from Pastel and Judge.

The afternoon sun shone on Hoku's glistening, golden coat. Darby had never seen anything more beautiful than her horse.

She climbed over the fence, leaving the halter and lead rope draped over it.

"Hoku!" she called.

The mustang filly lifted her head. Her ears pricked forward with interest.

Then, she deliberately turned in a half circle so that her hindquarters faced Darby, and went back to eating grass.

Wha...? Darby wondered.

Her horse had seen her and recognized her. So, what had *that* been about?

"Hoku," she called again.

This time the filly gave no sign she'd even heard Darby, but she must have.

"Come on, pretty girl," Darby coaxed, and Hoku walked several steps farther away.

All right. Not a problem, Darby thought.

Sometimes Hoku liked to tease, but there was one method that always worked when Darby needed to summon her. Darby had stumbled upon it completely by accident one day when she was tightening her ponytail. As soon as she'd lifted her arms and tightened the elastic, Hoku—who had been playing hard to get—came straight over.

Darby had been so amazed that she had tested it several times, and each time she tightened the ponytail, Hoku came to her.

The signal had never failed.

Darby clucked her tongue to get Hoku's attention. As the filly glanced back over her shoulder, Darby reached up and pretended to fuss with the elastic holding her ponytail.

Hoku gave a lovely, floating neigh, and for a moment Darby knew it was for her.

But she was wrong. Hoku was staring toward the ridge, where she'd seen Snowfire chasing Black Lava.

"You're not making sense, baby girl," Darby told her horse, and she strode closer, until she was almost near enough to touch Hoku.

With a disdainful snort, Hoku moved a few more long steps away.

Why hadn't it worked? Had Hoku even been watching when Darby made the ponytail signal?

"This is crazy," Darby murmured.

She walked to a nearby boulder, climbed onto it, and then, after another whistle, brought her arms up and pulled at her ponytail yet again.

Hoku kept grazing.

Sliding down from the boulder, she set off walking toward Hoku.

"Nothing in my hands," she said. "No halter and no rope."

No hay, either, she thought regretfully. But she couldn't help that now.

When she was within three yards of her horse, Hoku trotted another five or six yards away.

"Very funny," Darby muttered, hands on hips. "Hoku, come here, girl. Right this minute," she added, trying to sound stern.

If Darby's feelings were hurt—and they were headed in that direction—she couldn't let Hoku know it. Darby was the boss. Hoku was the horse.

"Nooo," Darby moaned quietly, because the horse had just broken into a lope and put the length of a football field between them.

Think like a horse, Darby ordered herself. She took a deep breath. As she slowly let it out, she tried to sink into Hoku's mind. Was the filly sad? Disappointed? Angry?

The last time I was with Hoku . . . Darby frowned, because it had been four days ago. Then Hoku had been happy to see her. She'd frolicked like a foal, and they'd leaned together like buddies.

Then Hoku had been heroic, facing down Black Lava to defend Darby. They'd seemed closer, more bonded than ever. What could have changed?

Okay, think, Darby, she urged herself. What had

happened *after* Hoku drove off Black Lava? Darby realized that the stallion was trying to capture 'Iolani Ranch mares, and she'd run up the path in order to tell everyone at Sun House.

And how was that different from other times Hoku had stayed loyally beside her?

Dummy! Darby scolded herself. Every one of those other times, Darby had petted and sweet-talked her horse, rewarding her loyalty, showering her with affection and gratitude.

This time Darby had run away and been gone for days!

"I messed up big-time, didn't I, girl?" Darby said, but she was talking to herself.

By the time Kit reached the pasture riding Biscuit, Darby was surrounded by horses munching grass, but none of them was Hoku.

The mustang had moved as far away as she could get, and looked attentively into Pearl Pasture, as if she could see other horses.

"She won't come to ya?" Kit guessed as he halted Biscuit alongside Darby.

Darby shook her head. "I'm not exactly sure what's wrong, but I have an idea."

Kit didn't ask for the reason. He bumped back the brim of his Stetson and studied Hoku. "She's mad at you, that's sure. And I could ride out, rope her, and drag her back, but that'll only make things worse. Don't ya think?"

"Yes," Darby admitted.

"Better call off training for today."

"What about letting her know who's boss and all that?" Darby questioned.

"That'll wait until you two are friends again."

"How do I make that happen?" Darby asked, trying not to sound as upset as she felt.

"I reckon she'll come around once she's shown you she's mad."

"How long do you think it will take?" Darby asked.

Kit shrugged. "Depends on the two of you. Does she want to be stubborn? You willin' to change her mind? It's just like with people."

"Should I bring her a treat?" Darby asked, trying to think of ways to make up with Hoku. "Jonah hates it when I give treats to the horses. He says I spoil them."

"I don't think an apple or carrot will hurt, but I'm not sure it will help, either."

Darby kept staring at Hoku until Kit asked, "Want to jump on behind and I'll take you back up?"

"Thanks, but I'll walk."

"That's a good plan," Kit said.

"It is? Why?"

"You're walking away from her this time, letting her miss you and regret her stubbornness. See ya back up there," Kit said, and Biscuit carried him away.

One more try, Darby thought as Kit trotted off.

She peered over the heads and backs of the other horses until she found Hoku again. *Just turn,* Darby silently willed the filly. *Then you'll see me tighten my pony-tail and you'll come over and I'll show you how much I love you and appreciate that you defended me against Black Lava.*

But Hoku didn't turn.

With a lump in her throat, Darby left the pasture.

Ann was just climbing out of her mother's car when Darby arrived at Sun House.

"Mal-a-sadas! " Ann shouted, pumping a fist toward the sky.

In the kitchen, Aunty Cathy had already plugged in her electric frying pan and poured vegetable oil into it.

"Be careful with the hot oil," she told them. "If this stuff splatters, it can give you a nasty burn. In class, don't let anyone sit too close to it."

"Not even Tyson," Ann promised, but Darby noticed her friend's fingers were crossed.

"Not even him," said Aunty Cathy, who had heard plenty of Darby's complaints about Tyson.

While the oil heated, Aunty Cathy set out milk, sugar, salt, eggs, butter, and yeast. They mixed the ingredients into a simple dough.

"Now, being very careful, get some dough on a wooden spoon and plop a lump into the hot oil. Not plop," she amended. "Ease it into the oil. Here, I'll show you how to do the first one, and you can do the rest."

Darby and Ann were both afraid of the sizzling oil, but they teased each other into trying it.

Slowly and carefully, Ann laid a ball of dough into the oil, then jumped back as it spit and hissed. She handed Darby the big spoon.

"Your turn."

"Do I have to?"

"Yep, the presentation's tomorrow. I think we've cut it about as close to our deadline as we can."

Darby scooped a ball of dough onto the spoon and stared at the bubbling oil.

"Just lay it down," Ann encouraged her.

"I'm just waiting for the right moment," Darby insisted.

"This isn't like catching a wave in bodysurfing. There is no right moment," Aunty Cathy said.

Darby hovered over the crackling oil, then dropped the dough ball in. Oil splattered up, burning her thumb, but she survived, and the next time her technique was better.

After the malasadas were cooked, they had to cool, and then they were rolled in sugar. After cleaning up, Darby and Ann took a plate of the warm, sweet treats to the living room for Jonah, Megan, and Aunty Cathy.

The girls dished a second plate for themselves and took it out to the lanai.

There they ate and planned their presentation, and once, while Ann was writing and Darby was staring off the lanai, Darby heard the strumming of a guitar.

Two guitars, she corrected herself. Cade and Kit were singing to Medusa, and Darby sighed. She remembered her first hours with Hoku and the days that followed. She'd sung Christmas carols to the filly.

Even before she'd adopted the sorrel mustang, Hoku had been hers.

But that seemed like a long time ago.

Chapter Eight

On Friday afternoon, Darby spotted Aunty Cathy waiting by the 'Iolani Ranch truck in the Lehua High parking lot.

"C'mon," she said, dragging Ann by the arm.

Finals were over. It was the last day of the school year. In celebration, Aunty Cathy had brought wonderful orchid leis for all three girls.

She placed the delicate strands of flowers around their necks and kissed their cheeks. By the time Ann saw that her camping gear was already stashed in the back of the truck, brought earlier by her mother, and she and Darby had climbed up into the backseat, Megan was already in the front seat talking about a beach party.

As Aunty Cathy pulled away from the school, she asked, "So? Were the malasadas a hit?"

"They were great!" Darby said.

"And the presentation was great," Ann said.

"And, of course, Ann was great," Darby joked.

"And Darby, well, there must be a word for her performance," Ann said, tapping her fingertip against her lips. "Oh, yeah, *great*!"

"So, Darby, was it great?" Megan teased.

"Yeah, it was okay," Darby played along. "We didn't spill anything or splash anyone with scalding oil."

"Even those who deserved it," Ann added.

"My voice didn't shake at all, and I was concentrating so hard on explaining, I forgot to be nervous." Darby slumped back against the seat, smiling.

"You look smug," Ann said as she leaned back against her curly red hair.

"Well, just to prove to you that I could have done that other presentation if we'd really had to, I'm going to sing you a song."

"Nuh-uh," Megan said, looking back at the younger girls.

Darby sang, "School's out, school's out, teacher let the mules out!"

She had no idea where the rhyme had come from, but it made everyone in the truck laugh, so who cared?

They weren't leaving on the camping trip until five o'clock, Jonah said, so the girls raced through lunch.

They wanted to get in their very first practice for the *keiki* rodeo.

"Jonah is counting on the rodeo to bring a lot of attention to the ranch," Darby said as she and Ann led Navigator and Baxter to the round pen.

Navigator walked behind Darby, never hanging back against the reins or surging ahead. She patted his shoulder in appreciation. She loved the trusty brown-black Quarter Horse.

"Attention's nice, but a little bit of money wouldn't hurt," Aunty Cathy joked as she joined them with Biscuit and one of the cremellos. "Isn't that right, Cash?"

"Mom, that's Pastel," Megan corrected as she came up alongside with Conch. The grulla was so excited, he trotted on tiptoe as she led him.

"Well, they should all be named for money," Aunty Cathy said. "You'd be just as happy as *Peso*, wouldn't you?" she asked the horse. "Because these *free* cremellos Babe gave us are costing us a fortune."

"Because they eat so much?" Megan asked.

"That, and we had to buy new tack, renovate the pasture, update their shots, and have them shod—you name it!"

"They'll earn their keep this summer," Darby reminded her.

"Let's hope so," Aunty Cathy said. "But things will be *great*," she emphasized, "if we can sell a few horses at the rodeo and Jonah can book Kanaka Luna with one or two mares. And it would be nice for you kids to win some prize money, too."

Even though the rodeo's prize money wasn't much, Darby had already been daydreaming about spending it on something nice for Hoku. She had to remind the mustang that she loved her.

She'd been thinking about horse shampoo, for a couple of reasons. It would not only smell nice, but every time Hoku caught a whiff of the scent on her mane, she'd remember Darby's gentle, massaging hands.

Of course, that assumed Darby'd be able to catch her someday.

Besides the fact that it would be fun to win, she wanted to prove to Jonah that she understood the realities of ranch life, and that his beloved 'Iolani Ranch would be safe with her, if he—

"The rodeo is going to be awesome," Megan's voice broke into Darby's thoughts, and Darby was glad.

"Too bad Sugarfoot can't compete," Ann said.

"No?" Aunty Cathy asked as she held the round pen gate open for the girls.

Ann shook her head. "He could use the practice, but he's too unpredictable."

Darby had heard about Sugarfoot chasing a client in a wheelchair and knocking him over. That wasn't what someone who'd come to the Potters' ranch for a therapeutic riding session expected, but Ann insisted that Sugarfoot's behavior was "a colt thing."

When Cade rode up on Lady Wong, Darby realized she hadn't asked him how Honi was doing.

"Is your mom's pony happy to be home?" Darby asked.

"She seems real happy," he replied. "And so does Mom. Tutu's keeping her busy learning stuff about herbs and all."

Darby nodded, and would have asked more, but Ann was ready to ride.

"So what are we practicing today?" she asked.

"Jonah's registered us for the ranching events, like trailer loading and sorting and doctoring," Cade said. "But he told me we could do more."

"We *have* to do the Gretna Green!" Megan insisted.

"What's the Gretna Green?" Darby asked.

"The real Gretna Green is a place in Scotland," Aunty Cathy explained, "a spot that's famous because young couples can elope and get married there without their parents' permission."

"But wait. How can they have a horse race based on that?" Darby turned to Megan, since she was so eager to compete in the event.

"In the race, the teams are made up of a girl and a guy, each on separate horses, and they have to hold hands while they race the other couples," Megan explained.

Cade shook his head. "They're just going for time.

It's not a free-for-all start."

"Holding hands!" Ann cried. "That still sounds crazy dangerous!"

"It can be," Cade put in. "You have to practice, know your horse, your partner, and, uh, what you're doing."

"I think Darby and I should enter the race," Megan suggested.

"I thought you said it was a guy-and-a-girl event," Darby reminded her.

"So what?" Megan countered. "Baxter and Conch look great together."

"But they're both sort of green," Darby protested. "I don't know."

"I'll show you how to do it. You can start on Navigator and I'll take Biscuit, since they're both so reliable."

"Okay," Darby agreed warily. She'd first learned to ride on Navigator and knew that, whatever happened, he wouldn't spook or do anything silly.

With Cade and Ann sitting on the top fence rail watching, Megan and Darby lined Biscuit and Navigator up side by side.

"Okay, take my hand and we'll start by walking," Megan instructed. She held out her left hand.

Darby did, but she felt off balance.

"Am I leaning too far?" she asked.

"No, but you're crushing my hand," Megan told her.

It was true. She'd been holding so tightly to Megan's hand, her fingers were already stiff.

"Sorry," she apologized with an embarrassed laugh. Then she loosened her hold, but didn't let go.

"That's better," said Megan. "You don't have to lean so far over. Our arms can reach."

Darby adjusted her seat, and she felt a surge of confidence.

"Take it to a jog," said Megan when she sensed Darby was ready.

Navigator swung into a jog, and so did Biscuit.

Both girls were smiling and soon were loping around the corral hand in hand.

When they came to a halt, Darby realized that her cheeks hurt from smiling so hard. "That was cool," she said.

Cade and Ann clapped and cheered from the fence.

"Way to go!" Ann yelled.

"Ready to try it on Baxter and Conch?" Megan asked.

"Why don't we just stay with Navigator and Biscuit?" Darby suggested.

"Because they're not the horses Jonah wants us to ride," Megan reminded her.

"And they're definitely not the horses we want to sell," Aunty Cathy added.

"That's for sure," Darby said.

"Baxter and Conch will be perfect for this," Megan said. "If you look at them, their conformation is a lot alike. They probably have totally matching strides."

"Okay," Darby said. She was a little embarrassed at her hesitation, but as Cade adjusted her stirrups, she found out he harbored some doubts, too.

"This is just for fun," he said, looking up at her. "If things feel wrong, let me know."

Mounted on Baxter and Conch, Darby and Megan started once more at a walk. Instantly Baxter stepped out, trying to stay ahead of Conch. Darby clung to Megan's hand, but just barely.

"Help," she whimpered, half laughing as she lost contact with Megan.

Megan urged Conch to keep up, and they tried it again.

This time Darby made a serious slip to the right as Baxter flattened his ears and Conch widened the space between them.

Megan did something to scold the horse, and Conch narrowed his distance from the other gelding. That worked until Baxter began forcing his tongue against his bit, trying to break into a run.

Darby didn't know how she was supposed to shorten the reins using just her right hand. Finally, she was stretched so far to her left, she had to decide whether to let go or be pulled out of the saddle.

Darby let go. When Megan circled back, she said,

"This stunt's going to need some work."

Darby nodded, but then she said, "Try it with Cade."

"Why?" Megan looked suspicious.

"Because he's about a zillion times better rider than I am, and if we want to sell these horses, we want someone riding who makes them look good," Darby insisted.

She and Megan rode over to where Cade and Ann sat on the fence.

"Those two are definitely not in sync," Ann said when they arrived.

"I'll say," Megan agreed, rubbing her arm. "At this rate one of us will wind up with a disconnected shoulder. Or dislocated. However you want to say it, one of us will pull the ball out of the socket joint. I saw it on that kinesiology handout."

"Are you totally set on entering this event?" Darby asked.

"Yeah," Megan replied. "Sort of. Definitely. Come on; we'll just have to practice."

Darby didn't want to take the hand Megan offered her, so she asked, "Cade, will you try it? You're a lot more experienced than I am. Maybe I would do better as part of a four-person team. I could ride Baxter in sorting, doctoring, and trailer loading, the kinds of things I'm a little more experienced at. That's what Kimo suggested."

"But, Darby," Megan protested.

"I'll just slow you down," Darby said, then gave Cade a pleading look Megan couldn't see.

"What do you think, Cade?" Megan asked.

"I'll give it a try," he agreed.

Darby realized that a hint of red had risen on Cade's cheeks, like a sudden sunburn. These cowboys were sure easy to embarrass.

 Chapter Nine

After an early dinner, Megan helped Ann and Darby wrap half of a fresh batch of malasadas for their camping trip.

"Jonah loves malasadas," Aunty Cathy said as she watched them.

Jonah patted his belly. "I love them too much. But I can't resist. Besides, I have another reason for wanting to take a batch along tonight."

"Another reason besides eating them?" Darby asked.

"You'll see," Jonah said mysteriously as he left the kitchen.

"Megan, I don't know why you won't come with

us," Darby urged. "It will be so much fun."

Megan laughed. "Oh, sure, I just love eating Jonah's poi and jerky for breakfast, lunch, and dinner."

"Is it really that bad?" Ann worried.

"Not if you're a fan of mashed taro root without a drop of salt or sugar."

Ann made a face.

"Just kidding. Sort of kidding," Megan said. "And it's not the *only* reason I'm not going, anyway," she replied. "Cade and I need the time to practice, because once you two come back we'll have to concentrate on the four-person team events."

Ann slid Darby a teasing glance, and Darby returned it. They'd already practiced right up until dinner.

"*What?*" Megan asked, realizing something was going on.

"You know *what*," Ann teased. "Cade and you just *have* to work together this weekend."

"Yes . . . we do," Megan insisted. "Excuse me if I'd rather not break Cade's arm by yanking him off Baxter. *Your* nickname is Crusher, not mine."

Ann and Megan had once both been on the soccer team at school before Ann had been sidelined by an injury, and they still acted like teammates sometimes.

"True," Ann agreed, laughing.

"Hey," Megan said, wagging her index finger at the other girls, "you just wait. If Conch doesn't get sold right out from under me, *then* you can say this was about Cade."

Darby, Ann, and Jonah parked the truck at the drop-off point at the foot of the trails to the Two Sisters volcanoes.

The drop-off point was sort of a staging area for trips up to the volcanoes. On the edge of the small parking lot there was a water spigot for filling canteens, a bulletin board for messages and announcements, and a sign-in sheet. This land belonged to Jonah and Aunt Babe. It had been given to them by their mother, Tutu, and an invisible border ran between the two volcanoes.

But Aunt Babe and Jonah agreed on two permanent rules: Everyone who went up toward the Two Sisters had to print their name on the sign-in sheet, and no one was allowed beyond the stone trees, which were two miles from the craters of the volcanoes.

Dusk hadn't fallen yet, but a mist in the air blurred the peaks of the twin volcanoes, making them look even more magical.

Darby rode Navigator at a slow and steady pace up the steep terrain. She had loaded her fanny pack with her flashlight, inhaler, some water, and a granola bar, all of which bumped along behind her as they rode.

Jonah was ahead of her on Kona, his big gray cow horse, and Ann was behind, rocking in the saddle with

Biscuit's steady gait. They passed ohia trees with blazing red blooms, also called Pele trees after the fiery goddess said to rule the volcanoes.

The last time they'd been up here, one of the Two Sisters had erupted. Darby tried not to think about it, but the Pele trees reminded her of Tutu's tale about the white stallion, who was only one of many forms that Pele's brother Moho could assume.

He was the god of steam, and another of Pele's brothers, who sometimes took the form of a black stallion, was the god of thunderclouds.

Snowfire, god of steam.

Black Lava, the god of thunderclouds.

It struck Darby as poetic that these two roamed together, just as they did in the legend.

"You girls are quiet," Jonah commented as he ducked to pass under a branch laden with low-hanging lehua blossoms.

"I guess I'm getting a little tired," Ann admitted. "That doctoring race—getting on and off of Lady Wong, who must be seventeen hands tall—"

"Sixteen," Jonah put in. "And you do a nice job riding her."

When Ann sat a little straighter in the saddle, Biscuit picked his feet up and arched his neck. Ann apparently knew how rare Jonah's outright compliments were, and her pleasure had flowed right down the reins to the buckskin.

They came to a trail Darby remembered from her

trip with Megan and Ann. It still gave her a shiver when she thought of how these trails were formed. They were carved naturally from flowing lava on its way downhill. If one of the volcanoes should erupt while they were on this path, they were in big trouble.

Volcanic signs were everywhere. There was a *kip-uka*, an island of fertile life surrounded by black lava rock. And this *kipuka* had a strange fernlike plant she'd never seen before. Huge and curled in on itself, kind of like a fuzzy green cinnamon roll, it reminded Darby of illustrated books she'd read that showed dinosaurs prowling among prehistoric plants.

Jonah stopped to look at it, too. "That's *moa*. The only other place you'll see that is on a fossil, yeah?" he told them. "Tutu uses it to make a medicinal tea for a condition babies get called thrush."

Farther on, Jonah pointed out tall, spindly koa trees. Dark, sickle-shaped pea pods dangled from their highest branches.

"Take a good look," Jonah said, pointing. "And not just because darkness is coming. Those koas grow only in Hawaii. We've always used them for war canoes and surfboards, but now the wood is used for high-priced furniture."

"And that's bad?" Darby asked.

"Only if you think native Hawaiians should be able to afford it."

When they'd ridden past the koa trees for about a mile, Jonah stopped and dismounted.

His gray waited, ground-tied, as Jonah unfolded his pocketknife and cut some branches from a tree with bright green leaves.

"What's that?" Darby asked as Navigator halted next to Kona.

"*Papala,*" he answered as he cut.

"For Tutu?" she asked.

"No, for us."

Even in the fading light, she saw her grandfather's smile. She hoped he could see well enough to enjoy this trip. She hoped they'd take it a dozen times more.

"They have such pretty little pink flowers," Ann noticed.

Sticking the branches in his pack and climbing back on Kona, he started them moving along the trail once more. "The flowers are pretty," he agreed. "That reminds me of a story about another flower: the *koali* morning glories."

"Are morning glories those blue flowers that grow on vines?" Darby asked.

"Yeah, but these are the wild kind," he clarified. "The flower opens blue in the morning and turns pink later in the day."

"Cool," Ann murmured.

"The Old Ones used the vines as ropes. When I was a kid, I had a swing made from it," he told them. "There's a legend, though, that the vine was inhabited by little worms that the Creator blessed with thought, then turned into people."

"Tyson must have been one of those people," Ann joked. "It's easy to believe he started life as a worm."

"Yeah, but there's that part about being blessed with thought," Darby answered, and Ann laughed.

 Chapter Ten

The sounds around the riders died out, until only one stubborn bird cried, "e-e-vee," as it trailed them for another mile.

Jonah stopped, peered around the clearing, and suggested that they take advantage of the last of the light to make camp.

Darby was glad she'd learned to do this before. Her fingers were as swift and sure as Ann's as they helped set up the horses' high line, tying each end of a long rope to nearby ohia trees as though they planned to hang out their laundry with clothespins.

Jonah set up his tent and the two-person tent Darby and Ann would share, while the girls watered and hand-grazed the horses.

"We got the best of the deal," Darby said as they watched Jonah fit poles together and pound stakes into the forest floor.

"Thank you," Ann called to Jonah.

He just waved and said, "Be careful. Make sure those horses are spaced apart. And don't give 'em enough slack to get a leg over the rope, or then you'll see a real rodeo."

"Speaking of that, I haven't seen any wild-horse tracks, have you?" Darby asked.

"It's too dark to tell," Ann replied.

"And our horses aren't restless," Darby said, watching the tied horses.

So Black Lava and his band weren't hiding from Snowfire on Two Sisters. They must have gone all the way back up to Sky Mountain.

After dark, Jonah and Ann helped Jonah build a fire with the wood they'd collected earlier.

All three of them stared into the crackling flames. Their color shifted from gold to orange to scarlet, reminding Darby of her filly's coat.

"The fire feels good," Ann said. "I didn't think I'd be cold."

"We've ridden up a couple thousand feet," Jonah said. "There's a reason the snow doesn't melt on Sky Mountain. Now you two aren't complaining about the extra blankets I made you pack, yeah?"

Jonah squatted by the fire, stripping one of the

papala branches he'd cut on the trail with his knife. "It's the altitude that makes it cold, but we're prepared for it."

Darby unwrapped the malasadas they'd brought for dessert. The fire and dancing shadows made the pastries even more of a treat. Ann passed one to Jonah and he took it, but then he did something strange.

Instead of gobbling it down like the girls were about to do, Jonah wiped the malasada's greasy surface on the sharp end he'd carved from a *papala* branch.

Darby scooted closer to the fire, wondering what her grandfather was up to. She caught her breath in surprise as he lightly tossed one stick up into the air, just above the fire. It whooshed up into the air like a flaming dart, before heading back into the campfire.

"Wow!" Ann exclaimed. "Did you know it would burn like that, Jonah?"

He nodded. "Ancient Hawaiians used *papala* branches for entertainment. They'd make spears of them, grease them, and then hurl them from the cliffs above the water. The wood was so light the flaming spears got caught by the trade winds and flew all over the place."

"I'd love to see that," Darby said. She pictured glowing sticks flying through the air, doing somersaults into the wind.

"If we were closer to the ocean I'd show off, but it's too dangerous to just throw flaming sticks around near these trees."

In the campfire's glow, Jonah's high cheekbones were shelves above dark hollows. When his heavy black brows lifted as though he'd just been struck with an idea, Darby thought it was a trick of the firelight.

But then her grandfather stood slowly. He looked around, judging his position on this mountain slope.

"If I remember right, there's a marsh near here. I can toss burning sticks over it, and the water will put out the flames."

"Awesome!" Ann cheered. "I never expected fireworks tonight."

Jonah held an already whittled handful of sticks. He handed them to Darby, then took a few uncut branches himself and told the girls to bring their flashlights as he lit their way with his own.

Darby and Ann walked through the darkness, following Jonah with confidence as he led them down a path leading away from their campsite. The girls playfully swung the beams of their flashlights through the darkness, pretending they were bright fairies.

"Ah, here it is. This way," Jonah said after a ten-minute walk.

They left the path and descended a slope. They'd gone down only maybe three yards before the slant leveled off into a marshy area. Damp earth squished beneath Darby's boots.

Jonah hung his flashlight lantern on a tree. The

marsh turned midnight green.

The night chitter of insects faded.

Jonah looked up. Darby looked, too, seeing that the break in the trees caused by the marsh exposed a sparkling mantle of stars against the night sky. The moon was a silver crescent.

A bird squawked in surprise, and Darby felt prickling along the nape of her neck. They were being watched. She was sure of it.

Let it be horses, Darby thought, not a wild boar and her piglets, or something cranky because they'd roused it from sleep.

Jonah took the malasada from his jacket pocket and used it to grease all the sticks. Then he took a slide-covered box of matches from his pocket. He lit the first match and then the first stick. As he hurled the flame-wrapped stick into the air, it went up, trailing yellow-orange streamers. But it was more dazzling coming down, a falling golden star attended by hundreds of red sparks.

"Better than Fourth of July!" Darby whispered, and the next stick Jonah threw flung off sparks of oil on its way up, then caught an invisible current of air and danced on the breeze.

"Wow," Ann said.

As the second stick drifted on its fiery course, Jonah launched another flaming stick and another, until three of the light wooden sticks were lifted, making firefly trails on the breeze.

"They're like balsa wood planes," Ann said. "Toby and Buck love those things."

"Same idea," Jonah agreed, and then, in rapid succession, he launched the first of the smaller sticks.

"Pele's happy," Jonah said as the sticks dipped and glided in the darkness.

Better than that, Darby thought, *Jonah's happy*.

A rising wind swept one swirling stick off course, away from the others. It sailed to the right, and Ann gasped as it plummeted straight down.

A sudden commotion, a thrashing in the tangle of shrubbery, and then dark forms rose. Darby heard a single, startled neigh.

Ann gripped Darby's wrist and whispered, "Wild horses!"

Ann was right. The herd had been hiding just yards away. No wonder she'd felt eyes following her.

Snorts and whinnies filled the night as the black forms thundered away.

"Aloha!" Jonah called after the horses. "*Papala* fireworks and wild horses! A great way to end our show, yeah?"

"You sure took us to the right place at the right time. Did you know they'd be here?" Ann asked.

"I'd like to say yes, but it was only luck."

Darby gazed at Jonah's happy face in the lantern light and didn't believe him. He might not have planned to find the wild horses in this way, not consciously, but his horse charmer's instinct had been at work from the first moment he set eyes on those *papala* branches and stopped to cut them.

No, it had started before that, when he told them to make more malasadas and bring them.

Then Jonah had led the girls to water, and, of course, the wild horses were nearby.

"Now that we've found what we came to see, let's go check our campfire and warm up the rest of those malasadas. I'd like to actually eat some," Jonah said, wiping his hands.

As they walked back to camp, Darby wondered if that had been Black Lava's herd. She was about to ask Jonah, when it came to her that such a question might crush his good mood. It would obviously remind him of his failing eyesight.

Later, she was glad she hadn't brought it up. The three of them were sitting by the campfire, eating malasadas, when Jonah said, "Don't worry, Granddaughter."

"I'm not worried."

"You are a little," he told her. "When I said we'd seen what we'd come to see, I could hear your bones stiffen in disappointment."

"No," Darby began, but Jonah laughed.

"Tomorrow we'll go back to the marsh and track them, see how they look in the sunshine. Now, please pass me another malasada."

"Okay," Darby agreed.

As she did, she was pretty sure that Kona's unhappy snort didn't mean anything. Neither did the sound of Navigator shifting from hoof to hoof, or Biscuit taking deep drafts of night air.

Chapter Eleven

The first gray rays of dawn woke Darby.

Beside her, Ann was curled down so low in her sleeping bag, only a tuft of curly red hair showed.

Darby fished in her backpack and pulled out clean underwear, socks, jeans, and a T-shirt. She squirmed down into her sleeping bag to change.

When Darby emerged from the tent, she was alone on the misty ridge where they'd set up camp. Last night's wood smoke scented the air, but that was the only similarity between this place and the site where she'd camped before, with Megan and Ann.

From this ridge she looked through a blanket of fog to see rolling hills and dark swaths of rain forest. Here and there a tree stood tall enough to pierce the densest gray. In the distance, Sky Mountain's peak rose through clouds.

Rustling in the nearby trees made Darby jump, but it was just her grandfather, arms loaded with wood.

"Good morning," he greeted her. "I didn't expect to see you up so early."

"And I thought *you* were still asleep," Darby said.

He shook his head, dropping the wood by the rock circle of last night's fire. "I wanted to get the fire going to have breakfast ready when you woke up, but since you're here you can help me start it. I'll show you how."

Darby crouched next to her grandfather as he demonstrated how to stack kindling into a little wooden hut. Until it caught, he wouldn't let her lay the heavier wood on.

"Make sure you stack it so that the air can circulate around it," he instructed.

"Are we having poi?" Darby asked, remembering what Megan had said.

He looked at her, surprised. "How did you know?"

"Megan told us you like to bring it on camping trips," Darby said.

Brown skin crinkled at the corners of Jonah's dark eyes as he coaxed the fire into life. "I'll bet she told you it was delicious, yeah?"

Should she lie or hurt his feelings? She didn't want to do either. "I don't remember what she said."

"You're a bad liar, Granddaughter," he said with a chuckle. "Mekana hates my poi because her mother loads it up with milk and sugar for her, and I make it the traditional way."

Jonah was right. Aunty Cathy's mashed taro root tasted a little like the instant oatmeal Darby used to heat in the microwave in California. It was stickier, but mostly she'd noticed its sweetness.

"When I was young, poi was so important to our people that whenever a bowl of poi was uncovered at the table, we believed that the spirits of our ancestors were with us," Jonah told her. "It was so sacred that any fighting among family members had to come to a stop while the bowl was on the table."

"That's a good tradition," Darby said.

"It is," Jonah agreed. "And since we were always eating poi, it made for a lot of peaceful meals. I recall times when your aunt Babe and I were fighting, but we had to stop to eat poi. After the meal we often forgot what we'd been fighting about."

When the fire was strong, Jonah began heating his pot of poi. The smell drew Ann from the tent. With eyebrows raised skeptically, she considered the bubbling white paste, then looked at Darby and asked silently, *Poi?*

Darby nodded.

"There are some 'ohelo berries on the bushes over there," Jonah said, pointing to nearby bushes dotted with berries that looked like a combination of a cranberry and a coffee bean. "Go pick them and you can toss some into the poi. They're sweet."

"Remember the last time we went camping and found 'ohelo berries?" Ann asked as she and Darby headed toward the bushes carrying their empty cups. "The horses went crazy for them."

"After we eat, let's pick some extras for them," Darby suggested. She glanced over at the horses. Kona's eyes were closed, and a back hoof rested on its point. The wild horses must have moved far enough away that he couldn't smell them anymore.

Before Darby poured the berries into her bowl, she scooped up a few and arranged them on a flat rock. Tutu had told her that 'ohelo berries were Pele's favorites, and though Darby didn't exactly believe in the volcano goddess, memories of a sky filled with red-hot boulders made her reluctant to skip the tradition.

Jonah's poi wasn't terrible, just bland, and adding the 'ohelo berries helped.

After breakfast they broke camp. Darby and Ann fed the horses and then gave them the berries, which they licked from the girls' palms before they could put them on the ground.

The girls saddled up, mounted, and watched to see which way Jonah would lead.

Jonah kept Kona at a walk as they moved over smooth pahoehoe. Of course the volcanic rock showed no hoof marks, but when they came to damp grass they took turns watching the ground. Darby still didn't see signs that horses had passed this way, but she noticed that the grass in the sun stood up straighter than the blades still in the shade.

Jonah gestured for them to follow him toward the marsh, and that was where they spotted the hoofprints of the horses they'd surprised the night before.

"We'll see if we track them to Sky Mountain," he explained. "They might've climbed higher to get away from us."

Darby was trying to remember the last time she'd ridden on slippery lava rock like this before, when Jonah slowed and pointed to the ground.

"Fresh tracks," he said. "Lots of them. Let's see if we can catch up." Jonah moved his rein hand just slightly and his gray stepped out, with Biscuit and Navigator right behind him.

Darby had such faith in Navigator's good sense, even the fast pace over steep terrain didn't frighten her.

After following the tracks for about a mile, Jonah slowed Kona, then halted. Her grandfather held out his left arm and sighted along it.

"What's up?" Darby asked.

"The tracks veered off, then just disappeared. They could've gone over that slab of rock, but not if they're headed for Sky Mountain."

"Maybe Snowfire surprised them," Darby suggested.

Kona lifted his black-gray muzzle and flattened his

ears. Then he danced his front legs forward and back.

Darby and Ann exchanged excited glances, and then looked to Jonah. He pressed Kona's neck with one hand, telling the horse to settle down, then turned back toward the marsh.

Before they reached it, Jonah took Kona up a trail that overlooked a swath of green grass. Kona neighed again, sounding even more agitated than before.

Darby smothered her gasp. A large herd of horses grazed below them. On a small rise of earth, just high enough to give him a view of the many colored mares and foals, stood Snowfire.

As Jonah motioned for them to move back, he whispered, "If you can see them, they smelled you ten minutes ago."

Keeping low, they left the trail, dismounted, and led their mounts. Darby planned the placement of her boots, watching for scree that could make her slip, fall, and cause a commotion.

They used trees and bushes for cover, and either they did a good job, or Snowfire didn't mind their presence.

The majestic, broad-chested white stallion was pure *kanaka*, a native Hawaiian whose lineage was undiluted by tame horses because his herd had always lived at such a high altitude.

As they watched, Snowfire left his solitary position, following a narrow path, then leaped down to confront a young bay stallion. The bay had lowered his head in a snaking motion, trying to persuade a mare to take directions.

Snowfire snorted, then aimed a kick at the young stallion, and his message was clear: If the young stallion didn't stop flirting with Snowfire's mare, he'd be kicked out of the herd.

The bay looked a little surly as he obeyed, then blew through his lips and began to graze with two red dun fillies.

Darby waited for Snowfire to chase him off once again, but this time the lead stallion didn't seem to care. He gazed at the youngster, but then returned to his grazing.

"He's not chasing him away from those females. I wonder why," Ann whispered.

Jonah shook his head. "Those fillies are probably his daughters, or too closely related to make good broodmares for his herd."

"So, what happens?" Darby barely breathed the words.

"Some rival stallion will steal them," he answered. "Snowfire will pretend to protest, but he'll let it happen."

"Then why hasn't Black Lava already stolen them?" Ann whispered.

With a slight but precise movement, Jonah pointed out four mares who stood a little apart from the others. One dun was a bright yellow, which reminded Darby of sulfur, and the others were shades of gray, from charcoal to nearly white.

Darby recognized the mares just as Jonah said, "I bet Black Lava was more interested in taking back his own mares, and that's why Snowfire drove him all the way down to the ranch."

 Chapter Twelve

*L*ater that day, once they were back at the ranch and Ann had gone home, Darby brushed Navigator and Biscuit, cleaned their feet, and turned Biscuit loose.

"Just a little longer," she told Navigator. "I have to keep trying."

The big Quarter Horse looked at her with wise eyes, emphasized by the rust-colored circles surrounding them, and yawned as she tied him by his neck rope within reach of a fresh pile of hay.

Darby showered the campfire smoke from her body and hair, then returned to Navigator.

"We're going to try something new," she told the horse, then led him over to the side hill. Bouncing on her toes, she managed to launch her middle across

Navigator's bare back, then pull herself on and up.

Using only the gelding's neck rope to guide him, she rode bareback, carefully, down to see Hoku in the lower pasture. She caught sight of her filly as they got closer.

Hoku grazed with the other horses, but she remained on the outskirts of the group. Somehow, she was still on her own. In the afternoon sun, her coat glinted with a coppery luster.

Darby felt the same jolt of love that she experienced each time she looked at Hoku. She had to win back the filly's trust.

Darby rode farther down the trail to the broodmare pasture, shifting from the right side of Navigator's spine to the left with each of his steps.

"For a big horse, you don't feel like you have much fat on you," she told him.

She stopped Navigator outside the gate to the pasture, but she didn't go inside. She sat on Navigator for two minutes before Hoku lifted her head, ears forward. The mustang's attentiveness lasted only for a second.

Again Hoku turned her tail in Darby's direction.

"Why are you so stubborn?" she muttered, but she didn't give in to her frustration. Hoku had to see her strength if Darby was going to turn this situation around. In her jeans pocket she had a packet of the 'ohelo berries she'd brought with her, remembering how Hoku had gobbled them up the last time they'd ridden near Two Sisters.

Hoku's vanilla tail swished as she grazed near a bay mare named Honolulu Lulu.

Had the two become friends? Just as Darby had wanted to fit in when she first arrived at Lehua High, did Hoku want to be part of this horse herd?

But she also loved Darby. Deep down Darby knew it was true.

Hoku never would have challenged a full-grown stallion like Black Lava, with no thought for her own safety, if she hadn't been devoted to Darby.

"It's just a big misunderstanding," Darby told Navigator, but she didn't tell him that both their hearts were hurting. "Thanks for doing your part, big boy."

Darby slid off Navigator, removed his neck rope, and gave him a gentle swat, turning him loose as she climbed the fence and made her way past the other horses toward Hoku.

The mares and foals glanced up with mild interest. Maybe they caught the scent of 'ohelo berries in her pocket, or maybe they just wondered why she'd become such a frequent visitor here.

She spoke to some of them, stroking their manes, recalling a time when Jonah had instructed her to ride Navigator in Hoku's presence in order to make the filly jealous.

She started out petting an old bay gelding named Judge, then ended up hugging him.

He gave a low *huh, huh, huh* sound, almost a

chuckle, and a sidelong glance told Darby that Hoku was watching.

Darby reached in her pocket, extracted a single 'ohelo berry, and fed it to Judge. This caught the interest of several horses, but only Hoku felt entitled to walk up to Darby and investigate.

Darby's heartbeat accelerated. It wasn't easy to stay with Judge instead of running to her filly to say she was sorry. But she did it, weaving her fingers through Judge's coarse black mane, working out tangles as she found them.

Let her come to you, she thought. She pretended to be oblivious to Hoku's slow, curious advance.

"Judge, when you were born in a barn in Nevada, did you ever think you'd end up here? Neither did I."

Darby fed Judge another berry and petted his muzzle. Hoku was so close, Darby could feel the heat quaking from the mustang's body.

"But I don't think we'll talk to her just yet, do you, Judge? You've been the good boy all along, and you deserve—"

In the next second Darby was bounced off her feet. Hoku rubbed her face on Darby's back so roughly she pushed her forward, and Darby fell against Judge.

Darby turned and looked at Hoku. She didn't care that it was a push. Hoku was paying attention to her again!

"Don't let her do that to you!" Jonah yelled sternly. She whirled around to see him across the pasture, sitting on Kona, watching.

Without even asking, she knew from things he'd said in the past why he was correcting her so firmly. Hoku was treating her as if she were another horse. That wouldn't lead in the direction they needed to go for training. They could be friends, but Darby had to be the one in charge.

"No," she told Hoku, hoping to sound firm, but not harsh. "Don't push me."

Hoku stared back, her brown eyes glittering with confusion. She whinnied nervously, champing her jaws.

"Be nice," Darby said mildly. She reached into her pocket, about to offer a handful of berries, but she was too slow.

Hoku had already whirled around, angrily offering her rear view.

Darby longed to soothe her horse's wounded pride with kind words, stroke her neck, and hand-feed her, but she was too aware of Jonah's watchful eyes.

He wouldn't approve of her kissing up to her own horse, and no matter how much she hated it, he was right.

As she walked away, Darby heard Hoku begin pacing, puffing with agitated breaths. *Please follow me,* Darby thought with silent desperation.

But the sound of Hoku's movements became more distant, and with a sinking heart Darby realized Hoku was not only *not* following her, but putting distance between them.

Darby continued walking in Jonah's direction for almost two minutes before she couldn't stand it any longer and sneaked a quick peek over her shoulder.

Two minutes must have been as long as either of them could stand, because when she glanced back, she caught Hoku looking over her own shoulder. Their eyes met, and then they both turned away.

Darby couldn't help it: She heard hoofbeats and, once more, with her heart aching, she turned back again, longing to see Hoku running toward her.

But the sorrel mustang was running in the opposite direction, away from her and toward the herd of tame horses, where she knew exactly who she was and how to act.

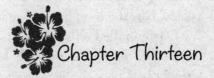

Chapter Thirteen

If it had been up to her, Darby would have slept in the next morning.

But no one slept late on a ranch. She had Pigolo's pen to clean, water troughs to scrub, and rodeo skills to practice.

Plus, if she got up now, she could play with Pigolo and Francie. Since she'd taken over their feeding, she'd also been their main playmate. It was so easy to make them happy. When she scratched Pigolo just above his tail, his closed mouth curved into a smile. When no one was watching she let Francie suck a bit of her shirttail, and the timid goat gazed up at her with adoring eyes.

Darby's feet had just hit her bedroom floor when she heard tires rattle over the cattle guard down by the highway. A really big vehicle crunched along the gravel road. Finally the tires stopped in front of Sun House, and Darby heard the yank of a hand brake.

Peach led the dogs' barking welcome, and Darby looked out her bedroom window.

The candlenut tree hid the vehicle, but she heard voices. Kit, she thought, and maybe Cricket.

Darby pulled on sweatpants and a T-shirt, but she didn't take the time to brush her hair into a ponytail. If Cricket was here, it meant news. Darby couldn't wait to find out if it was good or bad.

When she opened the front door, still in her bare feet, Darby saw Cricket leaning on the hood of a big truck, talking to Kit. A four-horse trailer was hooked on behind.

Darby didn't hear shifting hooves or anything that indicated there were horses inside. What she did notice was that Cricket looked more relaxed than any-time Darby had ever seen her.

Darby wasn't really eavesdropping, but when Cricket said, "Black Lava," Darby didn't miss it.

"What about Black Lava?"

She sprinted about six steps toward Cricket and Kit before tiny pebbles poked her into slowing down and choosing where to put her tender feet.

Kit and Cricket looked only a little surprised by the interruption.

"Somebody has big ears," Cricket said with a smile.

"Sorry—Ow." Darby stopped and lifted each bare foot to brush off its sandy sole. "But, you know . . . I'm really interested."

That was an understatement, and they all knew it, but Cricket just nodded. "I know. Here's what's up: Black Lava and his herd tried to take a shortcut through Hapuna this morning."

"What?" Darby gasped. The black stallion had run in a different direction this time. He must be getting even more desperate.

"Luckily, the pastor of a church on the outskirts of town is an early bird. He was just driving into the chapel lot when he saw them moving through the mist. He said it gave him quite a shock, since he'd prepared a sermon on the Three Horsemen of the Apocalypse—"

"I forget," Kit interrupted. "Do they bring the end of the world or something?"

"Were the horses okay?" Darby asked at the same time.

"No—I mean, yes. Wait, let me just . . ." Cricket gestured for both of them to let her talk. "The pastor spotted them drinking from a park fountain and decided they were just wandering horses. So he got back in his car, blew his horn, and drove slowly after them, herding them back toward Sky Mountain."

Darby swallowed hard. Things were getting worse instead of better.

"Cheer up," Cricket told her. She touched the

temples of her glasses and set them straight. "The bad times are almost over for Black Lava and his herd."

"Really?"

"The Wildlife Conservancy finally called me back. Their biologist went out with the Health Department guys and tested the water. Rain from the last few storms has improved the quality of the water in Crimson Vale. It's now potable."

"That means it's drinkable?" Darby checked.

"Yep," Kit said.

"Yes!" Darby shot her arm into the air, and her excitement set the dogs barking again.

Kit and Cricket laughed. "Would you like to ride with us to bring Black Lava's herd home?" Cricket asked.

"Are you kidding?" Darby yelped. "So that's what the trailer's for? We're all going?"

"I had a feeling you'd say yes, and I thought Jonah or Megan might want to come, too. And if you'd like to have Ann come along, we could use another strong rider."

"Definitely," Darby agreed. "But, hey, Cricket?"

Shyness closed in on Darby, but Cricket didn't rush her. She just raised her eyebrows.

"I know rescuing animals is what you do and all, but if you hadn't kept bugging the conservancy," Darby said, "who knows what could have happened? Thanks so much."

Cricket shrugged as if it were no big deal.

"She's pretty good at this stuff," Kit said, and Cricket blushed.

"I'll go tell Megan and call Ann, okay?"

Darby had sprinted halfway back to Sun House when Kit shouted, "Meet us back here at ten."

"We'll trailer the horses up to the drop-off and ride in from there," Cricket added.

"Okay," Darby said, then made a shaka sign in their direction, and kept running until she reached the front door.

Since she smelled pancakes, Darby expected to see Aunty Cathy, but when she bounded in to make her announcement, Megan sat alone, eating pancakes while she read a mystery novel.

Darby skidded into the kitchen, coming to rest with one hip against the table.

"Guess who gets to help escort Black Lava and his herd back to Crimson Vale?" Darby asked.

"Me!" Megan shouted.

"Maybe," Darby teased, then repeated the news Cricket had just told her.

"This'll be such good practice for the herding events at the rodeo. Too bad Cade went to Dee's place last night to help her patch the roof."

"At least the three of us can practice," Darby said.

She dialed Ann's number. While she waited for someone to answer, Darby rolled up a pancake, then bit a piece off. She watched Megan carry her plate to the sink and wash it, eager to get going.

After ten rings, Darby hung up the phone.

"No one's there," she told Megan. "Speaking of that, it's awfully quiet around here, too. Where is everybody?"

"It's Kimo's day off. I told you about Cade, and my mom and Jonah went to church."

Darby thought that over for a minute. It wasn't going to church that surprised her; it was the break in the ranch's routine.

"Mom just left me a note," Megan said as she headed for the front door. "I'm going to change. Be right back."

Most Sundays in Pacific Pinnacles, Darby and her mom had gone to church. Darby's favorite part had been singing hymns with neat old words and lots of verses. She'd hold the right side of the hymnal while her mother held the left and they'd both have fun singing together.

Weird, Darby thought suddenly. She'd never felt like a terrible singer in church.

Since she'd been at 'Iolani Ranch, no one had driven into town to any church.

She kept wondering what had changed as she tried reaching Ann again.

Just as she was about to hang up, Ann's father answered. He sounded breathless.

"Did you call before?" he asked. "Sorry. I was helping Ann and Ramona get off on a trail ride."

"Ann's gone?" Darby asked. Her friend would be

so sad she'd missed the chance to ride with the wild horses.

"Yep," Ann's dad said. "They're workin' the kinks outta Sugarfoot. Or tryin' to."

Darby didn't leave a message. Ann would hear what she'd missed soon enough.

Still, Darby thought as she hurried to her room to change into riding clothes, it was possible that Ann and her mother would ride in the same direction. Darby crossed her fingers and hoped so.

Cricket was on her cell phone, talking to another volunteer rider, when Megan and Darby came back outside.

"Pinwheel's a super mare, but we're taking all geldings. Believe me, you don't want to ride a mare into the territory of two warring stallions," Cricket was saying as Darby and Megan passed by.

They were ready to jump on the four-wheeler and go down to the pasture to catch Conch and Navigator when they saw Biscuit tied to a ring at the tack room, and Kit leaning against the corral fence, watching Medusa.

The steeldust mare stood on the far side of her corral. Head lowered, she glared at Kit through her black forelock.

"At least she's looking at you," Darby said. She couldn't help thinking of Hoku's tail-turning trick.

Kit shook his head slowly. "It's the *way* she's lookin'

that's got me a mite jumpy."

Darby and Megan both laughed until Medusa began trotting. Kit pointed and said, "Now watch this."

Medusa looked like a windup toy as she circled the corral. Her glare was gone. She didn't look left or right, or notice when she passed the three humans.

"That doesn't look healthy," Megan said. "I mean, like, mentally healthy."

"She reminds me of a caged zoo animal," Darby said.

"That's just what I thought," Kit said. He pushed back from the fence and began saddling Biscuit. "Maybe a break from my staring will help."

Then Kit glanced at the four-wheeler. "While you're down there, could you get Navigator for Cricket?"

Darby caught her breath, but Megan elbowed her, so she just said, "Sure."

Megan drove the four-wheeler and Darby sat behind with the lead ropes.

After they'd started, Darby leaned forward and said, "I wanted to ride Navigator."

"Don't be a baby," Megan shouted.

Of course Megan was kidding, but it didn't make Darby feel better. "I really only trust Navigator around wild horses," she said.

"You should be riding Baxter for rodeo practice, anyway. I'm riding Conch," Megan pointed out.

"That's not the same thing." Darby held tight as

Megan hit a bump in the trail.

"Cade worked with him for hours yesterday. Baxter will do fine," Megan shouted.

"I hope so," Darby said, and when Conch, Navigator, and Baxter surged toward the pasture fence at the sight of the girls, Darby was comforted by their eagerness.

The horses were haltered and trotting behind the four-wheeler in minutes, and Darby felt proud to be holding the lead ropes of three beautiful horses. The blue roan, grulla, and coffee-brown Quarter Horses were eager for work.

"Reporting for duty, huh, guys?" she shouted to them, and when six ears slanted forward to listen, Darby was happy all over again that she lived on this ranch.

The horses were saddled and loaded by ten o'clock, and since the truck had an extended cab, Megan and Darby sat in back.

As Kit pulled the trailer slowly down the road, he said, "I hope Jonah and Cathy're home soon. I don't like to leave my mare alone. She's likely to do something loco."

"Kit, I can handle this without you," Cricket said. "I told you that. I've got these two, and three volunteers. Add me in and that's six riders."

Megan and Darby stayed quiet. Kit and Cricket weren't really arguing, but Kit clearly wanted to be in two places at the same time.

❖ ❖ ❖

When Kit stopped the truck at the drop-off on the road below the Two Sisters volcanoes, Darby shivered. It was a six-mile climb to the very top, but no one was allowed up that high. Riding or walking beyond the stone trees was *kapu*.

Darby's shiver turned into an idea. Her gaze traveled up the slope to Two Sisters.

When she and Ann had ridden up here with Jonah, just the day before yesterday, they hadn't seen the stone trees. They'd veered west, toward the marsh.

Darby covered her eyes, hoping she could focus better that way. She heard doors slamming and Megan bumped her shoulder, but she had to think about the first time she'd come up here with Megan and Ann.

It had been the night before and the day of the eruption. But why was that important to finding Black Lava?

"Everybody's getting ready to go. We're the only ones sitting around," said Megan, who still sat beside Darby in the truck's cab. "Are you okay?"

Darby took her hands away from her eyes and tried for a reassuring smile.

"I'm fine, but remember when we were up here before?"

"No, Darby," Megan said, "almost getting buried alive in hot lava is such an everyday thing for me—" Megan broke off her sarcasm. "You have this hypnotized look in your eyes. I'm used to it, but you might freak out the volunteers."

Darby opened her mouth to answer Megan, but she kept remembering the steep terrain, one lava rock formation that looked like lion's paws, and another that looked like a stone pulpit. And the lava tube. Cool, dank, and strange, but somehow familiar.

"Darby, yeah, I remember that day." Megan jostled her shoulder. "What about it?"

"I don't know. That's what I'm trying to figure out." Darby looked up the slope again.

She'd just been here with Ann and Jonah on Friday. Why was it important to remember her earlier visit?

"Well, you need to either get a grip or a revelation, because it's time to get going," Megan said, and then both girls climbed out.

Kit had already unloaded their horses, and while Darby went to tell Baxter what was going on around him, Megan greeted people. When Megan waved a greeting to Lisa Miller, Darby did, too. Lisa was an animal lover and a friend of Cade's mother, Dee. Darby had met Lisa when they'd both volunteered at the rescue barn.

"What a beautiful horse," Lisa called to Darby.

Baxter knew the compliment was for him. He stepped toward Lisa, and only Darby, shortening her reins as she reached for the stirrup, then swung into the saddle, reminded him he was here to work.

"You're a good boy," Darby told Baxter, turning him toward the trail.

They were delayed when a man named Elliot arrived with a dancing chestnut mare named Pinwheel.

Folding her arms, Cricket reminded him that no mares were allowed on their rescue roundup. Wild stallions could be unpredictable, and taking a mare into their territory was asking for trouble. Still, Cricket said, the volunteer could take over communications if he and Pinwheel stayed behind with a CB radio and an extra-heavy-duty satellite phone.

Smiling at Cricket's calm authority, Darby thought: *role model*.

In only a moment, though, her attention shifted to Pele's trees. They were a clue, but she wasn't getting it.

They began riding. Cricket gave directions, and Megan talked with Lisa Miller as Darby tried to figure out what was bothering her.

It was the bird with the call like an old-fashioned radio dial whirling past a bunch of stations that made her remember Pigtail Fault, the strands of volcanic glass called Pele's hair, and the lava tube.

The first time she'd stepped inside, the coolness and scent had reminded her of Black Lava's hiding place behind the Crimson Vale waterfall.

Of course, Darby thought. Pursued by Snowfire and blocked at every attempt to go back to Crimson Vale, he'd found a place where he could hide. And it smelled like home.

Darby turned in her saddle and beckoned urgently for Megan to bring Conch up alongside Baxter.

"This is all beginning to make sense," she whispered to Megan. "I know why Jonah and Ann and I couldn't find Black Lava and his herd yesterday. I know where they were."

"Where?" Megan asked, lowering her voice to match Darby's.

"The lava tube. It's the closest thing to home that he could find, and there's that *kipuka* with a nice meadow nearby. Don't you think?" Darby asked when Megan hesitated.

"It's worth checking out," Megan said. "But I'm not sure we should share this with everyone else." She considered the other riders.

"But we can't just go galloping off on our own without some kind of explanation," Darby said. "I mean, that's what I want to do, too, but Cricket's so organized."

Behind them, horses shied. Hoofbeats approached, and when Lisa Miller's bay gelding backed into a tree, she muttered, "What does he want now?"

"Here comes our excuse to get out of here," Megan said. She grinned at Darby as Baxter began tossing his head and whinnying.

Pinwheel and her rider bolted into the group, and when Elliot pulled back on the reins, Pinwheel slid to a dead stop, but Elliot continued—sliding down her neck, over her head, and hitting the ground.

Some volunteers muffled their chuckles, but Darby wasn't one of them.

Baxter wanted to buck. He wasn't breathing like a scared horse. He was excited.

"Kit," Megan called to the foreman, "we're going to go on ahead with Baxter, or we're going to have two wrecks going on."

Kit had been riding forward with Cricket, ready to take a forceful stand with Elliot, but he looked back over his shoulder. Darby could tell he was thinking about Jonah's command that his granddaughter not ride alone into a herd of wild horses.

But she'd be with Megan, and Darby saw Kit take in the two of them. When Baxter loosed an earsplitting neigh, Cricket said, "If it were up to me, I'd let them. I trust those two."

"Go ahead," Kit told them. "But be smart."

"Let's hit it," Megan said, and Conch ran in place for a few steps, feeling her enthusiasm.

To Darby's surprise, Baxter didn't mind leaving the other horses. Together with Conch he headed out easily, and Darby thought she sensed a spirit of cooperation.

His muscles slid smooth and relaxed as he kept pace with the grulla.

"Baxter's happy." Darby smiled at Megan, even though she knew she'd better keep a wait-and-see attitude.

"Want to go faster?" Megan asked. It didn't quite sound like a dare.

"How fast?"

"Gallop?" Megan suggested. "Can you handle that?"

"You're on," Darby agreed, and Baxter gave a snort of anticipation.

"Here we go!" Megan shouted, and she'd barely lifted her reins when Conch rocketed into a run.

Baxter swung in behind the grulla. Satisfied to run in second place, he flashed his ears in all directions, taking in the new sounds around him.

This is what I love, Darby thought. Her body shifted with Baxter's and her fear flew away.

Darby saw Pigtail Fault, a crack in the earth that was yellow-lipped with sulfur. As they galloped past, a waft of vapor from inside the earth followed them like a sigh.

The stone trees were ahead, but Megan led left, past the formation that reminded Darby of lion's paws.

Hoofprints marked the trail all around them, but Darby noticed that the brittle threads of Pele's hair, on the right side of the path, didn't seem to have been shattered.

Megan had led Boy Scout troops and other youth groups on hikes to the lava tube, so Darby decided she'd follow Megan's advice on whether they went inside or not. Even though she remembered that the tube wasn't creepy and tight—in fact, she thought Megan had said it had a twelve-foot ceiling—she wasn't sure she wanted to be inside with a herd of wild horses. Ann had slipped on the smooth, wet lava rock floor before.

Megan didn't draw rein until they reached the mouth of the lava tube. Water dripped inside, and the horses' heads turned, as they listened.

Baxter's skin shivered from the sudden change in temperature as cool air blew toward them.

"I'm going to go in just a little way," Megan said.

Darby held her breath, listening for the echo of hooves and the reverberating scream of a stallion. But neither came.

Megan backed Conch out of the entrance.

"No one home," Megan remarked. "But you were right: They've been here. See for yourself."

Baxter stepped gingerly to the mouth of the lava tube and took a few steps inside, but only as far as the wash of daylight lit his hooves.

Darby never would have guessed how delighted she'd be to see fresh horse droppings, but they were a sign not only that Black Lava and his herd were nearby, but that this was their hiding place.

"Back," Darby told Baxter. She held her reins tight and squeezed with her legs, and the blue roan backed up eagerly. The sunshine warmed her back as if she'd been inside longer. She sighed, then turned to Megan and blurted, "That stone pulpit."

Megan knew instantly what she was talking about, but she looked dubious.

"But that's where we saw Snowfire before. Do you really think Black Lava would go there?"

"It's the closest food and water," Darby said, then shrugged.

"If that's what your horse radar is telling you," Megan answered, "let's go."

The other volunteers must have ridden in a different direction, because there was no sign of them by the time Megan and Darby reached the bulge of pahoehoe they'd nicknamed the Pulpit.

A wide crack had fractured the face of the volcano directly across from them since the last time they were here, but the scene below them was just the same.

Exactly the same, Darby thought, because there was Black Lava. Once again the stallion was in a dangerous mood. Dusty and disheveled, he glared at them only briefly and trotted in a tight circle around his diminished herd.

Baxter and Conch didn't look at each other, but the two young geldings dropped their heads and crowded so close together that Megan's and Darby's boots knocked.

The black stallion was a fearsome sight, and that made it all the scarier when Snowfire appeared. He walked into the meadow with his large herd.

Black Lava didn't give Snowfire a moment for

strategy. This time there were no arched-neck battle rituals.

Black Lava screamed to the white stallion and rose into a challenging rear. He had only a few family members left, and he'd fight to the death to keep them.

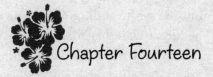 Chapter Fourteen

The white stallion thundered toward Black Lava. His head swung from side to side in a herding gesture.

"He's acting like he can just herd Black Lava. Isn't that . . . I don't know, an insult to another stallion?" Darby asked Megan.

"I think so, but . . . wow, he's not fighting! He's going after *another* mare!"

Snowfire charged right past Black Lava and slid to a dusty stop beside the bay mare, mother to the black foal.

Curious, she touched noses with the white stallion.

"Do you believe him?" Darby asked. "And her!"

Even when Black Lava changed direction and

whirled around to glare at Snowfire, the white stallion continued his flirtation.

Then Snowfire made a mistake. Considering the black foal, pressing against the bay's side, he flattened his ears and snapped at the colt.

The bay mare threw her head up and backed away, but the white stallion was determined to take her, and he didn't want her foal to come along.

"Why isn't Black Lava doing something?" Darby asked, because the black stallion had left the mare and foal to fend for themselves while he circled Snowfire's band.

"Look at him; he's deciding which one to steal!" Megan said.

It didn't take him long, but Darby couldn't stop looking between the two stallions.

In no more than a minute, Black Lava had gathered up two of Snowfire's gray mares, the sun-colored dun, and the two red fillies that Jonah had pointed out as Snowfire's daughters.

Nipping and squealing, Black Lava ran them back to his own herd. When one of the grays tried to return to Snowfire's band, Black Lava raced alongside her, refusing to let her leave.

Darby hoped the theft would distract Snowfire from bullying the bay mare, but it didn't.

"She's not going without a fight." Megan pointed as the bay mare thrust her body in front of Snowfire, protecting her baby while she kicked the stallion's forelegs.

Neither girl said anything. They knew that Snow-fire wanted only the mare, not the foal of his enemy. They knew that if he couldn't frighten the colt away, he would kill him.

Black Lava was ready to go. He circled his stolen mares and herded them before him, gathering the rest of his band along the way.

"Wait!" Darby yelled.

None of the horses noticed. The bay mare was still fighting Snowfire, and Black Lava was leaving her behind.

"I don't believe this!" Megan said, and her hand grabbed Darby's. They held on to each other so tightly their fingernails bit into one another's skin.

Finally Snowfire frightened the colt away from his mother's side.

"Run!" Darby screamed.

But the mare was exhausted, and the foal wasn't fast enough. A swing of the stallion's head sent the foal tumbling to the ground.

Snowfire loomed over him.

Darby didn't stop to think.

Whooping and yelling, she set Baxter on the down-hill trail and rode at the stallion.

"You're crazy," Megan shouted, but she urged Conch to follow the blue roan.

The sight and sounds of invaders made Snowfire halt his attack. He wheeled back to the mare and gave her rump a punishing bite.

Without a backward look for her foal, the bay mare galloped toward Snowfire's herd.

In the sudden quiet, the girls scrambled down from their mounts. Holding tight to their reins, since this was no time to test the geldings' willingness to stay ground-tied, they approached the black colt.

He flailed at the ground with his front legs, fighting back terror and exhaustion in an attempt to follow his mother.

"You can't," Darby said quietly.

The foal looked at her, dazed, and Darby handed Megan her reins. With every step she took, the baby looked bigger. He was probably three months old. She didn't want to scare him or hurt him, but she had to stop him.

When the colt bolted into an unsteady run after his mother, Darby didn't hear herself yelling or feel the tears streaming down her cheeks, but she tackled him to the ground and stayed on top of him until Kit came and helped them both to their feet.

Against everyone's better judgment, they'd decided to take the colt back to 'Iolani Ranch.

"He's hurt and scared, and he'll never survive alone." Kit had sounded disgusted as he finished loading the saddle horses and squeezed Darby and the exhausted colt into the truck cab.

Megan caught a ride home with the volunteer Elliot and his mare Pinwheel, because Cricket and the other volunteers were seeing that Black Lava and his expanded herd made their way safely to Crimson Vale.

Tired and terrified as he was, the black colt was not drained of energy. He whipped his neck back and forth and shoved his chest against the cage of Darby's arms, but she held on.

He stared up at the truck cab enclosing him and squealed for the blue sky to come back, and Darby just winced as the shrill sounds pierced her ears.

And he kicked.

"You're going to hurt yourself," she warned as his black legs, thinner than her forearms, struck out and hit the door, the gear shift, and Kit.

"Mighta been better off in back," Kit said, nodding toward the horse trailer.

They'd already been over this, so Darby didn't argue. They'd weighed the comfort other horses would have given the colt against the accidental trampling he'd get if he gave into his weariness and fell under their hooves.

"You're okay," Darby whispered to the colt. "We have other wild ones, where we're taking you. They'll speak your language, baby. It'll be the next best thing to home."

Even as she said it, Darby realized the foal had been on the move since birth, following his mother and Black Lava wherever they led. The little black horse had never known a real home, but maybe she could change that.

❖ ❖ ❖

"Not bad," Jonah said. "Doesn't mean we're adopting him, but not bad."

Arms crossed, he stood outside the round pen, watching Darby and Megan put Plan B into action.

Plan A had called for them to slip the black foal into Medusa's corral, but the steeldust mare had reacted to the noise of arriving trucks and horses with rage. She'd claimed the small territory of Hoku's corral as her realm and guarded the gate as if it were a drawbridge.

Even though she'd known the black foal in her wild life, it would be too dangerous to test her memory.

They had brought Hula Girl and her independent colt Luna Dancer up from the broodmare pasture to join the black colt. Even though they weren't wild, their presence seemed to soothe him.

The girls weren't having quite as much luck bottle-feeding him.

Aunty Cathy made sure Darby had washed her hands before she handed her a bottle full of milk replacer they kept for emergencies. Then Cathy joined Jonah, watching at the fence.

After their ride home, the foal wasn't as scared by Darby as by Megan, so Darby was the one to shake a few drops of the formula onto her hand, then smear it on the foal's nose and into his mouth.

Immediately his pink tongue appeared to lick at his nose. Once he'd lapped off all of the yellow-white formula, Darby applied more.

"Do you like that, Inky?" she asked.

"Inky?" Jonah asked.

"That's what we've started calling him," Megan explained. "Inky Dinky."

"Oh, honey, how's that going to sound when he's a magnificent stallion like his sire?" Aunty Cathy asked.

"Magnificent?" Jonah asked. "That troll of a horse?"

Megan ignored him and answered her mother. "I've already thought of that," she said. "He's going to be Black Lava's Inkspot."

"Yeah," Darby said with approval. She was stepping from side to side, trying to insert her milky index finger into the corner of Inky's mouth, but the foal kept backing into Megan as he tried to escape. "You have no idea what I'm trying to do," she said, "do you?"

"Dancer does." Megan laughed as the tame colt shoved his way in to lick Darby's fingers. When they were clean, Dancer licked Inky's milk-dotted nose.

Darby guessed that the black colt was used to the company of other foals, because he stopped ducking away and stood patiently as Dancer finished.

From Hoku's corral, Medusa neighed. Her tone had changed. Darby thought there was a questioning quality about it. Did the lead mare recognize the scent of a member of her old herd?

Twenty minutes later, Dancer was still the only one interested in the bottle.

"Inky's too old for the bottle. Let me get a bucket for him to try," Aunty Cathy said.

"But they're cute, and they like being bottle buddies." Megan pretended to pout.

"Not too deep," Jonah shouted after Aunty Cathy. "Wild ones don't like to put their heads in a deep bucket. They can't see what's sneakin' up on 'em."

Instead of a bucket, Aunty Cathy brought back a metal cake pan and told Darby to hold it at a slight angle.

It worked. Inky must have drunk from a creek or stream before, because he instantly understood. Though he managed to splatter about half of his formula on Darby, he drank three pans full of it.

When Kit walked back up from Medusa's corral to watch, he nodded at the colt and said, "Sorry, boss."

"What were you supposed to do?" Jonah said, and then, more pointedly, he added, "Besides, I'm gonna take his expenses out in trade from these two softhearted girls."

Darby smiled, even when Jonah shook his finger at her.

"Do you think Medusa recognizes his smell?" Megan asked as the girls left the corral.

"Hard to say," Kit answered. "She's settled down just a little, and she's interested; that's for sure."

The words were barely out of Kit's mouth when a commotion began down by the fox cages. Horsehide hit wood again and again. Medusa threw herself at the gate, reminding them she didn't like captivity, no matter what.

Chapter Fifteen

After nearly a week of hard practices, Darby was glad the day of the rodeo had finally arrived. On foot, she and Ann navigated their way through the crowd, and Darby took in her surroundings.

A rainbow arched over the Hapuna fairgrounds, its colors as vivid as the fluttering flags that decorated the site for the ranch rodeo. Tiny cowgirls in braids, wearing their own chinks and spurs, followed their big-sister cowgirls around. Experienced paniolos watched young riders warm up the mounts they planned to ride in the competition. Booths staffed by local clubs sold bento lunch boxes, mochi rice treats, malasadas, and cold drinks.

Darby was so nervous about her upcoming events

that it felt as though her insides were shivering, but Ann dragged her up into the stands to watch Megan and Cade compete in the Gretna Green race.

"C'mon," Ann said. "We'll have a better view from up here. We can sit with my family." She waved. "And here come Jonah and Cathy."

Jonah and Kimo had been working in the arena, going after loose calves and horses, then hazing them out of the competition area.

Kimo was still down there, and Darby was glad. Not that Megan had needed his help yet.

Megan had aced the barrel racing. She'd kept Conch so close as they wove between the barrels, it looked as if he touched them, but not a single one moved. The grulla didn't waste a step on nerves, and when they reached the end and turned to speed toward the finish line, the gelding lined out like a greyhound, and Megan's hat had flown off at the sudden burst of speed.

Best of all, she'd won first prize and set an arena record.

That was great, and it would certainly draw attention to 'Iolani Ranch horses, Darby thought, but she was still worried for her friend.

No matter how much Megan and Cade had practiced, the Gretna Green event looked dangerous to her. She was pretty sure it had to do with the whole ball-and-socket joint thing.

Below them, Kimo rode Cash. Kimo's hat was

decorated with flowers, and the cremello gelding glinted in the sun, prancing as if he were proud of the horseshoe-shaped lei that draped his neck.

Kimo glanced up and spotted Darby and Ann crab-stepping down the bleachers. He smiled and waved.

"Hey, Kimo!" Ann shouted down to him. "Cash looks great!"

"Baxter's looking good, too." Jonah nodded down to the arena, where Cade sat atop the blue gelding.

Darby felt a little tug of jealousy. Since Baxter's amazing calm during the stallions' confrontation, she'd liked the gelding even more.

"He's still green, but Cade's done a lot with him," Jonah went on. "I hope it's enough to impress a buyer."

"Conch, too," Aunty Cathy added. "He was amazing in the barrel race."

"He turned on a dime," Ann agreed.

"It wasn't all Conch," Jonah pointed out. "Mekana's good. Like her parents.

"You and that *pupule* Baxter are doin' okay," Jonah said, looking at Darby; then he leaned forward so that he could see Ann and her parents. "You, of course, are riding my best mare, so . . ." He shrugged as if Lady Wong were making Ann look good, and they all laughed.

So far things had gone very well. Besides Megan's first place win in barrel racing, Darby, Cade, Megan, and Ann had taken third in trailer loading and doctoring.

She only had sorting left to go, and Darby hoped Baxter's run in the Gretna Green race would help shake his sillies out. He loved working cattle and it showed, but sometimes he was a little too enthusiastic.

Cade would be riding Hula Girl, Ann would ride Lady Wong again, and Megan would be on Conch.

Jonah must have read her expression and guessed what she was thinking about, because he leaned close to Darby and said, "In the sorting, those two mares are a sure thing. They won't let those yearling calves blink without permission. Conch is doing good, too, and with calm horses all around him, even if he's not cowy, I think Baxter will do okay."

Just then an air horn blew, and the first contestants in the Gretna Green race sped into action. A brother-and-sister team, both on palominos, made a good start, but then a colorful cardboard box appeared from somewhere and tumbled across the arena. The palominos took off in different directions before reuniting.

When the riders stood up at the end, hand in hand again, and bowed to the grandstands, they got a standing ovation, but were disqualified from the event.

Next came a girl on a black-and-white paint pony and a boy on a taller bay.

"This is not gonna be pretty," said Ann's dad, and it wasn't. The air horn to start the race scared the children, and they stopped holding hands right after stepping over the starting line.

Then came Megan and Cade. The whole team wore 'Iolani Ranch colors—turquoise shirts and tan leather chinks over their jeans—but Cade and Megan looked especially great. And when the air horn blew, the horses took off on the same hoof.

From that step on it was clear that Megan had been right: not only did Baxter and Conch look great together, but their similar conformation helped them move in fluid togetherness. Fast and smooth, they made it possible for Megan and Cade to grip each other's hands without looking stressed or pulled.

"They look good together," Ann said in a teasing whisper.

"The horses or the riders?" Darby asked as the pair crossed the finish line.

"Both," Ann remarked, and Darby nodded.

In the next moment their time was announced, and they'd clearly won first place!

"Go, 'Iolani Ranch!" Aunty Cathy shouted, pumping the air with her fist.

From the arena Cade and Megan waved, but then Aunty Cathy and Ramona, Ann's mother, were pushing Ann and Darby.

"Only one more event until the sorting," Ramona said.

"You'd better hustle down there and help Cade check Baxter over. We want all our *keiki* and horses to look good," Aunty Cathy said.

Jonah stood and followed them. "Better than a

front-row seat, yeah?" he said as they walked down to the arena, but Darby wasn't so sure she wanted her grandfather watching her that closely. Their team was now tied for first place. Darby climbed onto Baxter just as she heard the announcer's voice.

"Since the time the first paniolo vaulted onto the first horse, working with cattle was transformed," it boomed over the loudspeaker.

"From the horses that swam the *pipi*, or cattle, out to the ships, to the horses that carry today's working rider, sorting one calf out of a herd has always been a primary responsibility.

"Cattle sorting requires skill, speed, and teamwork, and that's why we've saved this event for last."

Darby's fingers shook on Baxter's reins, but the blue roan didn't seem to notice. Although he still regarded the excitement around him with interest, it was clear the exertion of the games had settled him down.

Ann and Megan were joking around, but Darby listened intently as the announcer explained that the yearling cattle had numbers on their backs because one mounted team member after another would be required to move cattle in numerical order from the herd at one end of the arena across the line at the opposite end.

As the riders took turns sorting out their calf, the other riders would hold the herd at the line and keep the sorted animals from rejoining the herd.

"The team that sorts the most cattle in the allotted

time will win the event and, in this case, the *keiki* rodeo!"

They'd decided that Ann and Lady Wong would go first, then Darby on Baxter, followed by Megan on Conch, and finally Cade on Hula Girl. They didn't really expect to make such good time that they would be able to repeat the order, but they were ready to do it if they could.

Again they went last. A new group of yearlings was brought in for each team, and their small herd had the biggest variety of coat colors. Instead of all red calves, there were two black Angus, a cow that had markings like an Oreo cookie—at least that was how Darby saw him—and a kind of roan one.

This herd had been penned and waiting the longest. Their eyes rolled white as the wind kicked up and the flags fluttered crazily.

Everything started out perfectly, and Baxter took his turn as if he'd been working cattle his whole life.

"No biggie, huh?" Darby whispered to the gelding as soon as he'd moved the number two calf over the line, but Baxter just kept his eyes on the cattle. All at once he stiffened up and his ears pointed at the number six calf.

At first Darby was too busy watching Cade and Hula Girl perform to realize what Baxter had noticed.

Number six had a buckskin-and-gray coat, but the

two colors were intermingled like a milk shake in a blender.

"No way," she whispered to Baxter, jiggling the snaffle in his mouth to redirect his attention. "You can't think he looks like that cow with the crumpled horn."

Whatever he thought, Baxter couldn't keep his eyes off the calf, so when Cade's turn was over and they still had two minutes left on the clock, Darby was in the strange position of hoping Ann used every last second of their time. But she didn't.

"Like a hot knife through butter," the announcer boomed as Lady Wong sorted out calf number five in one minute. "Now let's see that little blue horse show us his stuff!"

"Go, Darby!" Ann shouted.

Darby set Baxter toward the herd at a controlled jog, but his head was lowered like a cheetah's as he headed for the buckskin calf. He wouldn't have gone after another calf no matter what the number on its back.

Luckily, the calf left his friends and moved ahead of Baxter at a fatalistic trot until Cade, staring at the clock, yelled, "Faster!"

Baxter and number six burst into a run at the same time, and because the air horn blew and their time ended as the calf crossed the line into the herd Megan and Cade were holding, their team won.

But that wasn't enough for Baxter. The blue roan

gelding had his heart set on catching the calf. While her teammates celebrated, Darby gathered her reins in tighter and tighter.

She was half-afraid Baxter would start bucking, and half-afraid he wouldn't. He had to stop! Instead he pressed forward even faster.

The calf looked back at him with wide eyes, spooked, and cut across the arena. Once he found an open spot in the fence, he darted through.

Baxter stopped, staring after the calf. Then, he sneezed. It was only then that Darby heard the laughter in the arena.

"Oh, well," she said, patting the gelding's hot neck. "At least they can't say you're not cowy."

Packed up and victorious, Jonah, Aunty Cathy, Megan, and Darby went with the Potters to a local steakhouse for dinner, while Kimo and Cade trailered the horses back to the ranch.

"I'll miss Hula Girl," Megan said as soon as they'd ordered. "Conch, too," she said with a sigh.

Hula Girl had been sold to a woman looking for a horse to use in competition. She'd been impressed by the chestnut's performance during the events, and by her sweet temper when she'd examined her later. Hula Girl showed none of the nerves or anxiety the woman expected from a mare who'd left her colt at the home ranch for the first time, so she paid for her on the spot and made plans to pick her up later that weekend.

Conch had gone to a polo coach from Hapuna Prep. The coach had been interested in Baxter as well, but ultimately decided that the blue gelding needed a little more work.

"He was right about that," Jonah said while the others laughed. "But he might make a cow horse yet."

As Darby ate her French fries, she heard Aunty Cathy talking to Ramona. "We did a lot of good for the ranch today, thank goodness. A man approached Kimo about buying Lady Wong, but Kimo's got him coming to see her foal, Black Cat, next weekend instead."

"And what did I hear about some Girl Scouts?" Megan asked her mother.

"Oh, yes! I spoke to a troop leader," Aunty Cathy told them. "Her girls want to work on a horsemanship badge, and I told her to think about coming to the ranch for lessons."

"The whole troop?" Darby asked.

"It's a small group, about seven," Aunty Cathy told her. "We can use Judge and the cremellos, maybe Navigator and Biscuit. They'd pay us, of course. The sooner those *free* cremellos can start earning their keep, the better."

"You've got that right," Jonah said.

After dinner, Jonah treated everyone to ice-cream sundaes. Darby was savoring her last bite of hot fudge when she realized how tired she was. But it was a good sort of tired, and she'd made a deal with herself to go down and visit Hoku the minute they got home.

They said good-night to the Potters outside the restaurant.

"It's strange that I won't see you in school on Monday," Ann said. "Come by next week and we can make a batch of malasadas, now that we're experts."

When they climbed into the truck, Darby and Megan slumped against each other, exhausted but satisfied with the day. At times like this Darby was so happy with her new life she could almost burst.

"You did good, sis," Megan said.

"You, too, sis," Darby replied.

Kit was waiting for them at the cattle guard.

The sun was just starting to go down, but Jonah had turned on the truck's headlights, and they spotlighted the foreman.

Darby's pulse had sprung into panic mode—she thought of Inky, Medusa, Hoku—but then she saw Kit's smile and she let out the breath she'd been holding.

"That was some sigh," Aunty Cathy said, looking back at her.

"Yeah, she woke me up," Megan said, yawning.

Jonah lowered his window, and Kit stepped up to talk to him.

"I think it'd be worth your while to walk the rest of the way in."

"I'm an old man," Jonah complained, but he'd already turned off the truck and was opening the door.

"Don't run," Kit cautioned as Megan and Darby started to. "Walk on your tippy-toes to Hoku's corral."

Darby had never heard Kit use a term like "tippy-toes." *He must be happy about Medusa,* Darby thought. That was really cool.

She worried a little as they walked past the round corral. At a quick glance the pen looked empty, but Inky was pretty small. He and Dancer were probably curled up together in a shadow.

Kimo and Cade stood watching the corral from the bunkhouse porch. The porch was just high enough to allow them to see over the fence. Darby couldn't wait to see what they could, so she rushed up the steps to stand beside them.

Of course, a week wasn't enough time to transform a horse, but Medusa looked like her old self, like she'd looked in the wild, before the tsunami.

Her pewter-gray coat, flecked with black, appeared soft as velvet. Her mane rippled in ringlets to her shoulder, and her forelock twirled down to her nostrils.

She raised one hoof, feathered with wispy hair, and moved with surprising care across the corral toward Inky.

She won't hurt him, Darby told herself. Kit wouldn't let that happen, and neither would anyone else standing there.

Everyone watched in silence as the two horses considered each other.

Medusa sniffed the black colt from nose to tail.

Remembering, Darby thought. *Medusa must be remembering they're family.*

"Been goin' on for over an hour," Cade whispered. "They keep following each other around."

When Medusa walked away from the colt, she crossed to the far side of the corral, and Inky followed her long tail, which was dragging on the dirt.

Then the mare did the last thing Darby would have expected: Upon reaching a patch of grass, Medusa lowered herself to the ground into a resting position, her front and hind legs folded, her head nodding.

Inky nickered. Medusa nickered back, and then the colt threw himself down on the grass beside her.

In about five minutes the only part of him not flattened in deep sleep was his tiny muzzle, which rested on Medusa's side as she dozed.

Kit turned to them all, not quite smiling, and Darby crossed her fingers.

Darkness had fallen by the time Darby made her way down the path to the broodmare pasture. Hula Girl stood near Luna Dancer, glad to be back with him. Lady Wong saw Darby and nickered a greeting.

"Are we buddies now that we've rodeoed together?" she asked the mare.

As usual, Hoku stood apart from the other horses. Darby knew her silhouette, and though shadows hid her flaxen mane, the moon was bright enough to pick out the white star on the filly's chest.

Hoku stood still, watching Darby, but not yet ready to forgive her. Still, Darby wasn't discouraged. If a wild mare like Medusa could make room in her heart for an abandoned colt, Hoku would remember she had room for one special human.

"*He puko'a ku noka moana*," Darby said. She was pretty sure she got her pronunciation right, and after asking Kimo, she knew what Jonah had meant when he'd said it to her.

Kimo said yes, it meant a rock in the sea, but that rock was standing up to the waves pounding all around it, and the saying meant the person it singled out wasn't stubborn, but determined.

Darby smiled into the darkness. She and Hoku could stand up to any trouble because they loved each other.

"I'll be here when you change your mind," she whispered to her filly, and then she blew her a kiss.

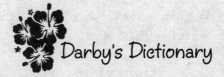

Darby's Dictionary

In case anybody reads this besides me, which it's too late to tell you not to do if you've gotten this far, I know this isn't a real dictionary. For one thing, it's not all correct, because I'm just adding things as I hear them. Besides, this dictionary is just to help me remember. Even though I'm pretty self-conscious about pronouncing Hawaiian words, it seems to me if I live here (and since I'm part Hawaiian), I should at least try to say things right.

ali'i — AH LEE EE — royalty, but it includes chiefs besides queens and kings and people like that

'aumakua — OW MA KOO AH — these are family guardians from ancient times. I think ancestors are supposed to come back and look out for their family members. Our 'aumākua are owls and Megan's is a sea turtle.

chicken skin — goose bumps

da kine — DAH KYNE — "that sort of thing" or "stuff like that"

hanai — HA NYE E — a foster or adopted child, like Cade is Jonah's, but I don't know if it's permanent

haole — HOW LEE — a foreigner, especially a white person. I get called that, or *hapa* (half) haole, even though I'm part Hawaiian.

hapa — HA PAW — half

hewa-hewa — HEE VAH HEE VAH — crazy

hiapo — HIGH AH PO — a firstborn child, like me, and it's apparently tradition for grandparents, if they feel like it, to just take *hiapo* to raise!

hoku — HO COO — star

holoholo — HOE LOW HOW LOW — a pleasure trip that could be a walk, a ride, a sail, etc.

honu — HO NEW — sea turtle

ho'oponopono — HOE POE NO POE NO — this is a problem-solving process. It's sort of cool, because it's a native Hawaiian way of talking out problems.

'iolani — EE OH LAWN EE — this is a hawk that brings messages from the gods, but Jonah has it painted on his trucks as an owl bursting through the clouds

ipo — EE POE — sweetheart, actually short for *ku'uipo*

kanaka — KAH NAW KAH — man

kapu — KAH POO — forbidden, a taboo

keiki — KAY KEY — really, when I first heard this, I thought it sounded like a little cake! I usually hear it meaning a kid, or a child, but Megan says it can mean a calf or colt or almost any kind of young thing.

kupuna — COO POO NAW — an ancestor, but it can mean a grandparent too

lanai — LAH NA E — this is like a balcony or veranda. Sun House's is more like a long balcony with a view of the pastures.

lau hala — LA OO HA LA — some kind of leaf in shades of brown, used to make paniolo hats like Cade's. I guess they're really expensive.

lei — LAY E — necklace of flowers. I thought they were pronounced LAY, but Hawaiians add another sound. I also thought leis were sappy touristy things, but getting one is a real honor, from the right people.

lei niho palaoa — LAY NEEHO PAH LAHOAH — necklace made for old-time Hawaiian royalty from braids of their own hair. It's totally *kapu*—forbidden—for anyone else to wear it.

luna — LOU NUH — a boss or top guy, like Jonah's stallion

mahalo — MAW HA LOW — thank you

malihini — MUH LEE HEE NEE — stranger or newcomer

mana — MAW NUH — this is a power you're born with. It's kind of a combination of instinct and intelligence.

māna — MAH NUH — I think to say this, you just hold the *ah* sound longer in your mouth and that makes sense. *Māna* means "knowledge you've gained from the mouths of others."

<u>menehune</u> — MEN AY WHO NAY — little people

<u>ohia</u> — OH HE UH — a tree like the one next to Hoku's corral

<u>pali</u> — PAW LEE — cliffs

<u>paniolo</u> — PAW NEE OH LOW — cowboy or cow-girl

<u>papala</u> — PAW PAW LUH — cool fireworks plant!

<u>pau</u> — POW — finished, like Kimo is always asking, "You *pau*?" to see if I'm done working with Hoku or shoveling up after the horses

<u>Pele</u> — PAY LAY — the volcano goddess. Red is her color. She's destructive with fire, but creative because she molds lava into new land. She's easily offended if you mess with things sacred to her, like the ohia tree, lehua flowers, 'ohelo berries, and the wild horse herd on Two Sisters.

<u>poi</u> — rhymes with "boy" — mashed taro root with the consistency of peanut butter. It's such an ancient food, Jonah says you're supposed to assume the ancestors are there when you eat it.

<u>pueo</u> — POO AY OH — an owl, our family guardian. The very coolest thing is that one lives in the tree next to Hoku's corral.

<u>pupule</u> — POO POO LAY — crazy

<u>tutu</u> — TOO TOO — great-grandmother

<u>wahine</u> — WAH HE NEE — a lady (or women)

Darby's Diary

Ellen Kealoha Carter—my mom, and since she's responsible for me being in Hawaii, I'm putting her first. Also, I miss her. My mom is a beautiful and talented actress, but she hasn't had her big break yet. Her job in Tahiti might be it, which is sort of ironic because she's playing a Hawaiian for the first time and she swore she'd never return to Hawaii. And here I am. I get the feeling she had huge fights with her dad, Jonah, but she doesn't hate Hawaii.

Cade—fifteen or so, he's Jonah's adopted son. Jonah's been teaching him all about being a paniolo. I thought he was Hawaiian, but when he took off his hat he had blond hair—in a braid! Like old-time vaqueros—weird!

He doesn't go to school, just takes his classes by correspondence through the mail. He wears this poncho that's almost black it's such a dark green, and he blends in with the forest. Kind of creepy the way he just appears out there. Not counting Kit, Cade might be the best rider on the ranch.

Hoku kicked him in the chest. I wish she hadn't. He told me that his stepfather beat him all the time.

Cathy Kato—forty or so? She's the ranch manager and, really, the only one who seems to manage Jonah. She's Megan's mom and the widow of a paniolo, Ben. She has messy blond-brown hair to her chin, and she's a good cook, but she doesn't think so. It's like she's just pulling herself back together after Ben's death.

I get the feeling she used to do something with advertising or public relations on the mainland.

Jonah Kaniela Kealoha—my grandfather could fill this whole notebook. Basically, though, he's harsh/nice, serious/funny, full of legends and stories about magic, but real down-to-earth. He's amazing with horses, which is why they call him the Horse Charmer. He's not that tall, maybe 5'8", with black hair that's getting gray, and one of his fingers is still kinked where it was broken by a teacher because he spoke Hawaiian in class! I don't like his "don't touch the horses unless they're working for you" theory, but it totally works. I need to figure out why.

<u>Kimo</u>—he's so nice! I guess he's about twenty-five, Hawaiian, and he's just this sturdy, square, friendly guy. He drives in every morning from his house over by Crimson Vale, and even though he's late a lot, I've never seen anyone work so hard.

<u>Kit Ely</u>—the ranch foreman, the boss, next to Jonah. He's Sam's friend Jake's brother and a real buckaroo. He's about 5'10" with black hair. He's half Shoshone, but he could be mistaken for Hawaiian, if he wasn't always promising to whip up a batch of Nevada chili and stuff like that. And he wears a totally un-Hawaiian leather string with brown-streaked turquoise stones around his neck. He got to be foreman through his rodeo friend Pani (Ben's buddy). Kit's left wrist got pulverized in a rodeo fall. He's still amazing with horses, though.

<u>Cricket</u>—is Kit's girlfriend! Her hair's usually up in a messy bun and she wears glasses. She drives a ratty Jeep and said, to his face, "I'm nobody's girl, Ely." He just laughed. She works at the feed store and is an expert for the Animal Rescue Society in Hapuna.

<u>Megan Kato</u>—Cathy's fifteen-year-old daughter, a super athlete with long reddish-black hair. She's beautiful and popular and I doubt she'd be my friend if we just met at school. Maybe, though, because she's nice at heart. She half makes fun of Hawaiian legends, then

turns around and acts really serious about them. Her Hawaiian name is Mekana.

<u>The Zinks</u>—they live on the land next to Jonah. Their name doesn't sound Hawaiian, but that's all I know.

Wow, I met Patrick and now I know lots more about the Zinks. Like, the rain forest—the part where Tutu told me not to go—used to be part of the A-Z (Acosta and Zink!) sugar plantation and it had a village and factory and train tracks. But in 1890, when it was going strong, people didn't care that much about the environment, and they really wrecked it, so now Patrick's parents are trying to let the forest take it back over. They hope it will go back to the way it was before people got there. I still don't know his parents' names, but I think Patrick said his dad mostly fishes and his mom is writing a history of the old plantation.

Oh, and that part Tutu said about the old sugar plantation being kind of dangerous? It REALLY is!

<u>Patrick Zink</u>—is geeky, super-smart, and seriously accident-prone. He looks a little like Harry Potter would if he wore Band-Aids and Ace bandages and had skinned knees and elbows. He says he was born for adventure and knows all about the rain forest and loves Mistwalker, his horse. He's not into his family being rich, just feels like they have a lot to pay back to the island for what their family's old sugar cane

plantation did to it environmentally. He likes it (and so do I!) that they're letting the rain forest reclaim it.

<u>Tutu</u>—my great-grandmother. She lives out in the rain forest like a medicine woman or something, and she looks like my mom will when she's old. She has a pet owl.

<u>Aunt Babe Borden</u>—Jonah's sister, so she's really my great-aunt. She owns half of the family land, which is divided by a border that runs between the Two Sisters. Aunt Babe and Jonah don't get along, and though she's fashionable and caters to rich people at her resort, she and her brother are identically stubborn. Aunt Babe pretends to be all business, but she loves her cremello horses and I think she likes having me and Hoku around.

<u>Duxelles Borden</u>—if you lined up all the people on Hawaii and asked me to pick out one NOT related to me, it would be Duxelles, but it turns out she's my cousin. Tall (I come up to her shoulders), strong, and with this metallic blond hair, she's popular despite being a bully. She lives with Aunt Babe while her mom travels with her dad, who's a world-class kayaker. About the only thing Duxelles and I have in common is we're both swimmers. Oh, and I gave her a nickname—Duckie.

<u>Potter family</u>—Ann, plus her two little brothers, Toby and Buck, their parents, Ramona and Ed, and lots of horses for their riding therapy program. I like them all. Sugarfoot scares me a little, though.

<u>Manny</u>—Cade's Hawaiian stepfather pretends to be a taro farmer in Crimson Vale, but he sells ancient artifacts from the caves, and takes shots at wild horses. When Cade was little, Manny used him to rob caves and beat him up whenever he felt like it.

<u>Dee</u>—Cade's mom. She's tall and strong-looking (with blond hair like his), but too weak to keep Manny from beating Cade. Her slogan must be "You don't know what it's like to be a single mom," because Cade repeats it every time he talks about her. My mom's single and she'd never let anyone break my jaw!

<u>Tyson</u>—this kid in my Ecology class who wears a hooded gray sweatshirt all the time, like he's hiding his identity and he should. He's a sarcastic bully. All he's really done to me personally is call me a haole crab (really rude) and warn me against saying anything bad about Pele. Like I would! But I've heard rumors that he mugs tourists when they go "off-limits." Really, he acts like HIS culture (anything Hawaiian) is off-limits to everyone but him.

<u>Shan Stonerow</u>—according to Sam Forster, he once

owned Hoku and his way of training horses was to "show them who's boss."

<u>My teachers</u>—

Mr. Silva—with his lab coat and long gray hair, he looks like he should teach wizardry instead of Ecology

Miss Day—my English and P.E. teacher. She is great, understanding, smart, and I have no idea how she tolerates team-teaching with Coach R.

Mrs. Martindale—my Creative Writing teacher is not as much of a witch as some people think.

Coach Roffmore—stocky with a gray crew cut, he was probably an athlete when he was young, but now he just has a rough attitude. Except to his star swimmer, my sweet cousin Duckie. I have him for Algebra and P.E., and he bugs me to be on the swim team.

❦ ANIMALS! ❧

<u>Hoku</u>—my wonderful sorrel filly! She's about two and a half years old, a full sister to the Phantom, and boy, does she show it! She's fierce (hates men) but smart, and a one-girl (ME!) horse for sure. She is definitely a herd girl, and when it comes to choosing between me and other horses, it's a real toss-up. Not that I blame her. She's run free for a long time, and I don't want to take away what makes her special.

She loves hay, but she's really HEAD-SHY due to Shan Stonerow's early "training," which, according to

Sam, was beating her.

Hoku means "star." Her dam is Princess Kitty, but her sire is a mustang named Smoke and he's mustang all the way back to a "white renegade with murder in his eye" (Mrs. Allen).

Navigator—my riding horse is a big, heavy Quarter Horse that reminds me of a knight's charger. He has Three Bars breeding (that's a big deal), but when he picked me, Jonah let him keep me! He's black with rusty rings around his eyes and a rusty muzzle. (Even though he looks black, the proper description is brown, they tell me.) He can find his way home from any place on the island. He's sweet, but no pushover. Just when I think he's sort of a safety net for my beginning riding skills, he tests me.

Joker—Cade's Appaloosa gelding is gray splattered with black spots and has a black mane and tail. He climbs like a mountain goat and always looks like he's having a good time. I think he and Cade have a history; maybe Jonah took them in together?

Biscuit—buckskin gelding, one of Ben's horses, a dependable cow pony. Kit rides him a lot.

Hula Girl—chestnut cutter

Blue Ginger—blue roan mare with tan foal

<u>Honolulu Lulu</u>—bay mare

<u>Tail Afire (Koko)</u>—fudge-brown mare with silver mane and tail

<u>Blue Moon</u>—Blue Ginger's baby

<u>Moonfire</u>—Tail Afire's baby

<u>Black Cat</u>—Lady Wong's black foal

<u>Luna Dancer</u>—Hula Girl's bay baby

<u>Honolulu Half Moon</u>

<u>Conch</u>—grulla cow pony, gelding, needs work. Megan rides him sometimes.

<u>Kona</u>—big gray, Jonah's cow horse

<u>Luna</u>—beautiful, full-maned bay stallion is king of 'Iolani Ranch. He and Jonah seem to have a bond.

<u>Lady Wong</u>—dappled gray mare and Kona's dam. Her current foal is Black Cat.

<u>Australian shepherds</u>—pack of five: Bart, Jack, Jill, Peach, and Sass

<u>Pipsqueak/Pip</u>—little shaggy white dog that runs with the big dogs, belongs to Megan and Cathy

<u>Pigolo</u>—an orphan (piglet) from the storm

<u>Francie</u>—the fainting goat

<u>Tango</u>—Megan's once-wild rose roan mare. I think she and Hoku are going to be pals.

<u>Sugarfoot</u>—Ann Potter's horse is a beautiful Morab (half Morgan and half Arabian, she told me). He's a caramel-and-white paint with one white foot. He can't be used with "clients" at the Potters' because he's a chaser. Though Ann and her mother, Ramona, have pretty much schooled it out of him, he's still not quite trustworthy. If he ever chases me, I'm supposed to stand my ground, whoop, and holler. Hope I never have to do it!

<u>Flight</u>—this cremello mare belongs to Aunt Babe (she has a whole herd of cremellos) and nearly died of longing for her foal. She was a totally different horse—beautiful and spirited—once she got him back!

<u>Stormbird</u>—Flight's cream-colored (with a blush of palomino) foal with turquoise eyes has had an exciting life for a four-month-old. He's been shipwrecked, washed ashore, fended for himself, and rescued.

<u>Medusa</u>—Black Lava's lead mare—with the heart of a lion—just might be Kit's new horse.

<u>Black Lava</u>—stallion from Crimson Vale, and the wildest thing I've ever seen in my life! He just vibrates with it. He's always showing his teeth, flashing his eyes (one brown and one blue), rearing, and usually thorns and twigs are snarled in his mane and tail. He killed Kanaka Luna's sire and Jonah almost shot him for it. He gave him a second chance by cutting an X on the bottom of Black Lava's hoof wall, so he'd know if he came around again. Wouldn't you know he likes Hoku?

<u>Soda</u>—Ann's blue-black horse. Unlike Sugarfoot, he's a good therapy horse when he's had enough exercise.

<u>Buckin' Baxter</u>—blue roan in training as a cow horse and I can stay on him!

<u>Prettypaint</u>—used to be my mom's horse, but now she lives with Tutu. She's pale gray with bluish spots on her heels, and silky feathers on her fetlocks. She kneels for Tutu to get on and off, not like she's doing a trick, but as if she's carrying a queen.

<u>Mistwalker</u>—is Patrick's horse. She's a beautiful black-and-white paint—bred by Jonah! He could hardly stand to admit she was born on 'Iolani Ranch, which is silly. Her conformation is almost pure Quarter Horse

and you can see that beyond her coloring. And what he doesn't know about Mistwalker's grandfather (probably) won't hurt him!

Honi—Cade's mom's gray pony. Her name means "kiss" and she really does kiss. Cade jokes that his mom likes Honi best. He also says Honi is "half Arab and half Welsh and all bossy." And, she likes to eat water lilies!

Snowfire—an amazing mustang from Sky Mountain. He reminds me of Tutu's story about Moho, the god of steam—Pele's brother, too, I think—who could take the form of a powerful white stallion. Snowfire's conformation is like Black Lava's. He looks just as wild and primitive, and though they're about the same size, Snowfire just seems wiser.

❦ PLACES ❧

Lehua High School—the school Megan and I go to. School colors are red and gold.

Crimson Vale—it's an amazing and magical place, and once I learn my way around, I bet I'll love it. It's like a maze, though. Here's what I know: From town you can go through the valley or take the ridge road—valley has lily pads, waterfalls, wild horses, and rainbows. The ridge route (Pali?) has sweeping turns that almost made me sick. There are black rock teeter-totter-looking things that are really ancient altars and a SUDDEN drop-off down to a white sand beach. Hawaiian royalty are supposedly buried in the cliffs.

<u>Moku Lio Hihiu</u>—Wild Horse Island, of course!

<u>Sky Mountain</u>—goes up to five thousand feet, sometimes snow-capped, sometimes called Mountain to the Sky by most of the older folks, and it's supposed to be the home of a white stallion named Snowfire.

<u>Two Sisters</u>—cone-shaped "mountains"—a borderline between them divides Babe's land from Jonah's, one of them is an active volcano.

<u>Sun House</u>—our family place. They call it plantation style, but it's like a sugar plantation, not a Southern mansion. It has an incredible lanai that overlooks pastures all the way to Mountain to the Sky and Two Sisters. Upstairs is this little apartment Jonah built for my mom, but she's never lived in it.

<u>Hapuna</u>—biggest town on island, has airport, flagpole, public and private schools, etc., palm trees, and coconut trees. It also has the Hapuna Animal Rescue barn.

<u>'Iolani Ranch</u>—our home ranch. 2,000 acres, the most beautiful place in the world.

<u>Pigtail Fault</u>—near the active volcano. It looks more like a steam vent to me, but I'm no expert. According to Cade, it got its name because a poor wild pig ended up head down in it and all you could see was his tail. Too sad!

<u>Sugar Sands Cove Resort</u>—Aunt Babe and her polo-player husband, Phillipe, own this resort on the island. It has sparkling white buildings and beaches and a four-star hotel. The most important thing to me is that Sugar Sands Cove Resort has the perfect water-schooling beach for me and Hoku.

<u>The Old Sugar Plantation</u>—Tutu says it's a dangerous place. Really, it's just the ruins of A-Z sugar plantation, half of which belonged to Patrick's family. Now it's mostly covered with moss and vines and ferns, but you can still see what used to be train tracks, some stone steps leading nowhere, a chimney, and rickety wooden structures which are hard to identify.

❧ ON THE RANCH, THERE ARE ❧
PASTURES WITH NAMES LIKE:

<u>Sugar Mill and Upper Sugar Mill</u>—for cattle

<u>Two Sisters</u>—for young horses, one- and two-year-olds they pretty much leave alone

<u>Flatland</u>—mares and foals

<u>Pearl Pasture</u>—borders the rain forest, mostly two- and three-year-olds in training

<u>Borderlands</u>—saddle herd and Luna's compound

I guess I should also add me . . .

<u>Darby Leilani Kealoha Carter</u>—I love horses more than anything, but books come in second. I'm thirteen, and one-quarter Hawaiian, with blue eyes and black hair down to about the middle of my back. On a good day, my hair is my best feature. I'm still kind of skinny, but I don't look as sickly as I did before I moved here. I think Hawaii's curing my asthma. Fingers crossed.

I have no idea what I did to land on Wild Horse Island, but I want to stay here forever.

DARBY'S GENEALOGY

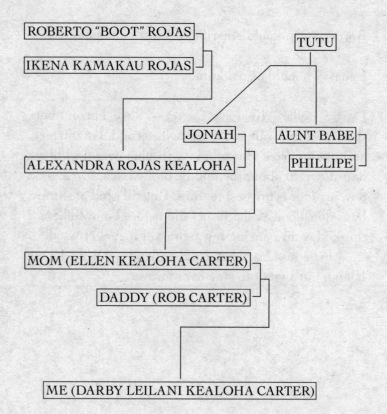

Darby and Hoku's adventures continue in . . .

FARAWAY FILLY

Faraway Filly

"Wake up, Darby Leilani."

A voice in the middle of the night was usually scary, but this one wasn't.

Blinking, Darby struggled up on her elbows and looked into her grandfather's face. His white robe hung askew over his shoulders. He squatted next to her bed.

"It's bright in here," Darby said.

"Horse thief moon, they call it," Jonah told her. "Don't want to scare you, but we've got one."

Did her heart understand his words before her head? Darby's chest filled with thudding.

Don't want to scare you.

That was frightening enough, but *horse thief*! Those

two words made her bolt up and swing her legs off the bed.

"Hoku!" Darby said.

Her grandfather made a disgusted sound as if no horse thief would want her mustang filly when there was a pasture of Quarter Horses to choose from. But he didn't say that.

"Go get Cade. That boy can see in the dark better than I can."

"Okay—"

"I don't just want to scare that thief away. I want to know who he is."

Owl eyes, her friend Megan called Cade, and though there was nothing supernatural about the young paniolo's ability to see in the dark, it was pretty amazing.

"Tell him, take the new ATV, the big one." Jonah made sure Darby nodded before he went on.

"I'm awake," she assured him.

"Tell Cade not to confront rustlers, yeah? Herd the horses away from the crook. Get a license number. That's it."

Darby's brain spun as Jonah left her room.

Just let some stranger try to put a halter on Hoku, Darby thought as she tugged on her jeans. Her wild filly would leave the guy spinning.

She grabbed a T-shirt and pulled it on.

Getting the license number would be tough, but she and Cade could tiptoe up behind the truck and—

"Tell Cade to be careful of the yearlings up in

Two Sisters," Jonah called from the hallway as Darby searched for socks in her dark room. "Don't want them colliding with each other or running into fences. Their brains haven't come in yet and they'll be *pupule* as—What are you waiting for?"

Forget the socks. Darby bolted through her doorway, down the hall and plopped on the bench by the front door. A row of shoes—from slippers to riding boots—were lined up there.

As Darby worked her bare feet into boots, Jonah opened the front door. The smell of wet grass came in, along with a curious "woof" from the dog run.

Darby was on her feet, eyes focused in the direction of the bunkhouse when Jonah's hand closed on her shoulder.

"Tell Kit to meet me at my truck. We'll take the road and cut 'em off while Cade comes up from the pasture."

Darby nodded once more, then burst into the June night. Overhead, the sky looked like navy blue velvet cloth on which someone had dropped a new dime.

Full moon. Horse thief moon.

To her right, the cremello horses moved across their pasture like a ghost herd. To her left, the bunkhouse windows were dark, but moonlight made its roof look like wet silver.

What time was it, anyway? The witching hour, she thought. Was that midnight or just sometime really late?

As she jogged, she decided maybe it was dark-thirty. Once, when she'd been little and her father had caught her reading in bed before sunrise, he'd told her to go back to sleep because it wasn't even dark-thirty yet.

She'd read that most people died between midnight and four. Was that because everyone else was sound asleep? Was that what the rustler was counting on? Well, he'd picked the wrong ranch.

She'd nearly reached the bunkhouse when she heard the dogs panting with excitement, wondering what she was doing.

"It's okay," Darby called to them, and when she glanced back, the bunkhouse lights were on.

The bunkhouse door stood open. Both Cade and Kit were dressed, but hatless and still hopping around, putting on boots.

"Jonah says we have a horse thief," Darby managed. Short of breath, she pointed vaguely toward the pastures. "We're supposed to take the ATV down and spook the horses into running away from him—the bad guy—and he—Jonah—will meet you"—she pointed at Kit—"at the truck."

Her feet had tried to keep up with the pace of her thoughts. Darby leaned forward a little, palms on her thighs, and tried to catch her breath.

Cade came onto the porch and before she could tell him she was fine, she saw he was staring away from her, over the dark pasture. Kit followed and stood, hands on hips, waiting.

No coddling, Darby thought. Unlike her mother, cowboys didn't make a fuss over her oxygen deprivation. Living on a ranch meant asking for help if you needed it. Right now, she didn't.

But Hoku might.

"Do you see anything?" Darby demanded.

Cade shook his head. "The guy must be good."

Darby realized none of them had questioned Jonah's warning. Whatever he'd heard or sensed, they believed him.

Her grandfather had been born on 'Iolani Ranch, just like many Kealohas before him. He knew the sounds and smells belonging to every minute of the day and night. If his instincts said the full moon was lighting the way of a horse thief, he was right.

Cade grabbed a flashlight from inside and hustled toward the newer and quieter of the two ATVs. Darby waited for him to get on, then threw a leg over the vehicle and crowded on behind him.

"Hey," he objected.

"If Jonah didn't want me to go, he would have told me to stay put. Call the police or something. Instead, he sent me down here." Darby wasn't certain she was right, but Cade didn't waste time arguing.

Darby took the flashlight he slapped into her palm. Before Cade switched on the key, Kit handed her a cell phone as he jogged past.

How was she supposed to hang on? Hugging her

legs to this thing like she would on a horse might not work.

"Hurry," Darby urged Cade, "before I have to carry something else."

But she really had another reason for making Cade hurry. She saw Jonah's outline near his truck. His hands were on his hips. Even though she couldn't make out his features, she'd bet he was glaring her way.

She gave Cade a push with the hand holding the cell phone.

"When did you get so—?"

"He could be after Hoku!" she snapped. "Go!"

They roared into motion, setting off a chorus of barks. As they zipped past the truck, Jonah shouted, "Stop!"

Cade couldn't have heard, because he kept going, concentrating on driving.

The distraction of Megan rushing out of her upstairs apartment, calling, "I wanna go!" was probably to blame for Cade hitting the rock instead of going around it. They stayed airborne for a few seconds before they touched down, banked right, and then sped down the path to the pastures.

"Give me a horse any day," Cade grumbled.

"That's for sure," Darby answered. A horse didn't want to crash on a steep dirt trail. A machine didn't care.

Although moonlight showed the way, Darby felt

disoriented for a minute.

Keeping her eyes open while she yawned, Darby saw they'd taken the trail that ended at Borderlands, the pasture for the saddle herd. At the approach of the snarling ATV, the horses scattered, mostly in groups.

As they came up on the stallion's compound, Darby watched Kanaka Luna's running shape. His dark mane and tail were carried on the breeze like gun smoke.

To the left, in the Flatlands, mares and foals drifted toward Pearl Pasture. They weren't moving in a panicky run, but they were reverting to wild instincts, fleeing danger instead of facing it.

So it was kind of weird, Darby thought, that Tango and Hoku, the only two horses which had actually been wild, didn't run.

Darby let out the breath she'd been holding. It made no sense, but she'd been certain the trespasser's intention was to steal Hoku. Even when she saw her half-wild filly standing so close to Tango that she could have been the rose roan's shadow, Darby wasn't convinced otherwise. Something told her Hoku was the thief's target.

She fought back the urge to call her filly to her. She longed to do it, but lately Hoku had been playing keep-away, and it was pretty embarrassing to be snubbed by your own horse.

Suddenly, though, Darby knew where the intruder was hiding. The horses were telling her.

Discover all the adventures on
Wild Horse Island!

HarperTrophy®
An Imprint of HarperCollins Publishers

www.harpercollinschildrens.com